For His Glory

RITA H. JOYCE

For His Glory

RITA H. JOYCE

THE WHITE HORSE OF THE APOCALYPSE

RITA H. JOYCE

PROLOGUE

Nestled in a green valley of the Northwest was a popular racetrack. A spectacular view of Mount Rainier, framed by manicured lawns, flower gardens and hanging fuchsia baskets afforded rest, relaxation and work for thousands of people. It's pavilions danced to the tune of young and old alike – watching and waiting for the sound of a bugle and the birth of pounding hooves leaping from the starting gate.

This is the story of a life of fascination with horses yet never imagining receiving an inspiration to buy a racehorse. I knew what its name would be, where it would be purchased, the design of the jockey silks, stable name and its ultimate purpose, all before any of it happened. That purpose would be revealed to many during a span of thirteen years as I trod the soil of the 'people rich' backstretch and its' environs.

You are invited to 'step into the skin' of ordinary and extraordinary horsemen and women involved in many facets of the racehorse industry. For most, the lifestyle is demanding, the wage gap incredible, yet unbelievable fulfillment awaits those willing to pay the price. Within these pages is a unique opportunity to share life BEFORE and AFTER racing as well as GLORY in the winners circle.

It is the author's desire in this memoir to acknowledge the thoroughbred racehorse and those God has assigned to bring these magnificent creatures to their fullest potential.

Rita Joyce

Note: This book was written before the racetrack referred to was torn down.
       A few years later a new one was built in a neighboring town.

ISBN: 978-1-963565-02-7 (Paperback)

Library of Congress Control Number: 2024909765

Printed in the United States of America

Published by

info@thequippyquill.com
(302) 295-2278

CONTENTS

CHAPTER ONE 1

    BEHIND THE STARTING GATE 1

CHAPTER TWO 5

    IT STARTED IN A PLUM TREE 5

CHAPTER THREE 11

    RACETRACK UNDER WATER 11
    ACTUAL NEWSPAPER PHOTOGRAPHS OF FLOOD 22

CHAPTER FOUR 23

    SWEET SIXTEEN 23

CHAPTER FIVE 31

    AN OUT OF BODY EXPERIENCE 31

CHAPTER SIX 43

    UM, I'M BEING INSPIRED TO BUY A RACEHORSE 43

CHAPTER SEVEN 51

    FOR HIS GLORY 51
    MY PASTOR BLESSING GLORY 58
    AN UNFORGETTABLE MOMENT OF GLORY GENTLY LIFTING UP
    MARNIE'S 3 YR OLD DAUGHTER 59

CHAPTER EIGHT 61

    FIRST RACE JITTERS 61

CHAPTER NINE 79

    CLOSE TO A MIRACLE 79

CHAPTER TEN 85

    FINALLY IN THE WINNER'S CIRCLE 85
    BUT SHOULDN'T BE 85

CHAPTER ELEVEN 95

    THE TWO-YEAR-OLD FUTURITY 95

CHAPTER TWELVE 97

    PATIENCE AND JUDGMENT 97

CHAPTER THIRTEEN 103

    MOVING ON - ANOTHER STABLE NAME 103

CHAPTER FOURTEEN 111

    THE HARD ROAD - VISION AT THE BARN GATE 111

CHAPTER FIFTEEN 119

    THE DREAM 119

CHAPTER SIXTEEN 121

    THE EVENING NEWS 121

CHAPTER SEVENTEEN 127

    FORGIVENESS AND DESTINY 127

CHAPTER EIGHTEEN 133

    A DREAM COME TRUE 133

CHAPTER NINETEEN 141

    A NEW STAR - REVELATION WHAT STABLE? 141

CHAPTER TWENTY 145

    RIDING GLORY - THE IMPOSSIBLE 145

CHAPTER TWENTY-ONE 151

    ANOTHER WORLD 151

CHAPTER TWENTY-TWO 161

    PEOPLE– ALMOST A SOAP OPERA 161

CHAPTER ONE

BEHIND THE STARTING GATE

With sweaty palms and shifting feet, two burly handlers coupled their hands behind 'For His Glory's' hindquarters. Their job was tough and dangerous-- forcing an uncooperative two-year-old toward the starting gate's number eight hole.

The now hushed crowd watched intently...waiting to see if precision timing and brute strength would allay the thoroughbred's fears.

'Glory', as he was nicknamed, refused to move.

All eyes shifted to the lead handler, a tall muscular man with unusually long arms. He had secured Glory's protruding chinstrap and painstakingly coaxed him forward.

Jockey Darryl Wyman smacked his boots against the dark bay's withers. "C'mon big Glory!" he urged.

Glory's ears snapped back, then forward. His eyes flashed, finally zeroing on the starting gate.

Anticipation mounted. Would our eleven hundred pound 'baby' submit or fight? I was afraid to wager...

Eventually loosening up, Glory crow hopped to the starting gate, much to the relief of the rear handlers. They were about to release him when he suddenly wheeled, scattering the help in all directions... one of the men stumbling badly.

Poised like a stallion, Glory tossed his head frantically, his thick black mane and serpentine tail magnified in the strong afternoon breeze. Wyman struggled to stay on his mount.

Out of the corner of my eye, I saw the lead handler grimace in pain. His right thumb became a casualty of his charge's unexpected burst of energy. Mumbling an expletive, the man reached into his pocket for a small rag and narrow leather strap. Wrapping the rag around his thumb and index finger--he waited for the jockey to bring Glory under control. Their eyes finally met.

"He's a cannon!" quipped Darryl.

"Crazy!" snarled the handler pointing to his makeshift bandage.

Glory momentarily froze, his huge eyes darting back and forth from the crowd to the starting gate. Relieved, the man stole the moment to loosen his rag.

I cringed, mindful of when a lunging rope 'wrapped' the fourth finger of my right hand. The painful throbbing lasted for three months!

Glory's once shiny coat was now frothing, characteristic of an extremely nervous first-time starter. 'Babies', as two-year-olds are lovingly referred to, are notorious for their antics, the worst of course, being able to unseat their jockeys.

With confidence quickly waning, I grabbed my husband's arm and scanned the rain threatened sky--seeking encouragement from above...

Nothing came.

Instead, insidious voices invaded my mind, refusing to be quieted. They screamed, "Glory won't make it! Accept the inevitable! Your dream will be aborted before its debut!"

Racehorses are allotted so many gate loads before being disqualified and sent back to the saddle area. Some never pass the test...never able to race...The thought was frightening!

The lead handler bit his upper lip and moved toward Glory. He ran the narrow leather strap through the chinstrap and secured it. The addition made for more flexibility and less chance for a repeat injury.

Meanwhile, the rear handlers moved stealthily, again clasping hands around Glory's tense body, repeatedly anchoring their feet in the soft damp soil.

Unfortunately, their gallant effort met with instinctive resistance. Glory lunged forward, again free from the hands of the three skilled gate crew workers.

I groaned, thinking this is worse than having a baby! Then again, this was a birth, the birth of a vision...

The gate crew attempted another load. I was suddenly aware of the tempter, the initiator of those infernal voices.

The evil one was challenging my faith...the belief that 'For His Glory' had a purpose and that nothing or no one could stop that purpose!

"You will not interfere!": I said authoritatively.

"It is still 'For His Glory' holding up the parade," bellowed the track announcer.

Glory's eyes glared as he approached the starting gate. Its narrow entry into stall number eight unnerved him. The regal bay tossed his head and challenged his commission. The eyes of the lead handler met those of his two aides and again they approached the nearly seventeen hand equine. The two anchored their feet firmly into the soft dirt and coupled their hands on the horse's hindquarters. Being already frightened, the alien presence on each side met with instinctive resistance. Glory lunged forward, out of the hands of the two skilled gate crew workers.

The lead handler managed to stay with him but even his efforts were thwarted when Glory suddenly wheeled, sending everyone running and our horse facing the opposite direction.

His black mane and tail flew in the cool evening breeze and his head tossed frantically, reminiscent of a stallion ready for battle.

Surprisingly, Wyman coaxed Glory, finally turning him toward the gate. He seemed to be cooperating. I squeezed my husband's hand even more tightly, hardly breathing.

With unrelenting heaves and heavy groans, the weary handlers applied their skills for what I deemed was their last try. Surprisingly, they muscled Glory into the number eight post position and slammed the tail gate shut.

The bell rang.

Twelve thoroughbred racehorses were off and running...

CHAPTER TWO

IT STARTED IN A PLUM TREE

Ellington Hill, 1948

The faint din of hoofbeats stirred me as I slept cozily beneath my pierzyna, a handmade comforter, made especially for me by my Polish grandmother. To keep warm in the chilly attic, I pulled the lumpy cover even tighter around my ears.

Annoyingly, the clip-clopping got louder and louder. My eyes popped open! Bouncing from the black iron-framed bed, I grabbed a stool and peered out the cupola window.

A beautiful palomino, about the color of my hair, trotted by. Mesmerized, I studied its golden body... like seeing something incredibly beautiful for the first time.

But why was the horse on Ellington's main road to town? Only cars tootled down the narrow dirt road and there was plenty of room on the pedestrian path.

As the rider pulled his horse to a walk, his spiffy tan outfit caught my attention. Could he be in a parade? I thought.

Unable to resist knocking on the tiny window, I waved at the horseman. He just kept going. It was hard to tell whether he heard my knocking or just chose to ignore me. The duo soon disappeared beyond the giant fir tree at the end of my grandparents' property.

Shivering, I grabbed a robe and ran to the window at the other end of the attic. I was not going to miss another glimpse of the palomino.

"Yuck!" I said aloud, quickly knocking a cobweb off my sleeve. Adding to this distraction was a terribly musty smell. That may be because the room was only used to dry green walnuts or cousins visited from Portland or Yakima.

When I parted the window's dusty white curtains, my eyes were drawn to snowy Mount Rainier. It gleamed on the horizon like a giant soft ice cream cone. The thought made me chuckle.

I could barely see the palomino and its rider when they finally appeared. Unfortunately, within a few seconds they disappeared over the hill.

Then came the overwhelming desire to ride this people carrying creature. Yes, I just had to ride a horse...

"Time for breakfast!" called Grandma Veronica, from the foot of the stairway.

"Grandma, I just saw the neatest horse!"

"Tell me about it later," she answered.

I quickly dressed and descended down narrow wooden stairs to the savory smell of Polish sausage.

My Grandpa John, a short man with sparkling blue-gray eyes and balding sandy hair, was shoving kindling into the wood and coal range. He lifted me up, knowing how much I liked hearing the crackle and pop of burning wood, especially as it flamed up when dropped onto hot coals.

Meanwhile, Grandma stirred a pot of steaming hot mush and made toast. Her old black teakettle whistled loudly on a back burner.

"Did you see the Palomino, Grandpa?" I asked excitedly.

"No," he said with a sigh. "I'm busy keeping the fire going. It took all morning to chop and stack this wood."

"Can we get a horse, Grandpa?"

"Niema," he replied matter-of-factly. My little ears did not want to hear the word "no." I knew a few words in Polish and niema definitely meant no!

Pestering Grandma might be a better option, I thought.

"Yes, I saw the horse, Renee. The boy was dressed pretty fancy, like he was riding in a parade... but it's the wrong time of year."

"Grandma, can I have a horse?"

Before answering, my heavyset gray-haired grandmother grabbed the kettle and poured Grandpa a cup of hot water. He stirred in instant coffee and added canned milk, lots of it!

I watched intently, waiting for Grandma to say yes. "We have a cow, chickens, rabbits, and Tommy, our great mouser. That's enough!".

"Ahhh..." I said sadly, but was determined to keep asking.

I walked to the kitchen nook, stood up on a bench and looked out the window, pondering.

Though Grandma was a very gentle person, she had definite opinions about animals. I figured that's because she had to kill rabbits and chickens for dinner. One day I accidentally went out after she chopped the head off a chicken and it was still running. Ugh! I could not imagine doing that job!

"Where are you going tonight, Grandma?" I asked.

She pointed to her curling iron warming on a shelf.

"It's Friday, you know, and there's a dance at the Polish hall tonight. Your Mom will pick you up early."

I always went home on weekends and returned to my grandparents house on Sunday nights. That's because my Mom worked long hours and so did my Dad. I liked going home but loved staying with my grandparents more.

"Breakfast is ready. Now let's eat," they said.

I squeezed into the right side of the nook, next to Grandma. She poured steaming cereal into two large blue bowls and then a smaller one for me. Grandpa John preferred the left side of the nook, where he routinely read the morning newspaper.

Waiting for Grandpa to say grace, I took a spoon and made valleys in my cereal. It was fun watching the mush ooze back in.

"Let's say grace," said John, folding his hands. "Bless us oh Lord and these thy gifts which we are about to receive, from thy bounty through Christ our Lord, Amen."

"Amen," I answered.

As Grandpa ate, something caught his interest in the newspaper.

"We need to be informed," he suddenly blurted out.

I waited for my grandfather's words. I knew they were important even if I didn't always understand their meaning.

Wiping his mouth, he turned to me.

"Look what Winston Churchill is saying about Poland! Remember Renee, we came from Poland and I'm thankful for America, God's great country. Do you understand? Well, when you get older..."

"But Grandpa, I'm five years old," I said with as much authority as I could muster.

"You will understand more when you get older. Just remember to be thankful for everything," he repeated.

I shook my head, wishing I could grow up fast!

After the meal, Grandpa readied himself for his job at the ironworks foundry while Grandma gathered clothes for washing. I headed outside.

Crisp air greeted me as I sprinted down the back porch stairs. The lowest branch of the front yard's giant fir tree was my goal. I gripped it tightly, swinging with gusto, striving to hit the north side of Grandpa's stand-alone single car garage, about twenty feet away. Inside was 'Darwin', the family named car. As usual, my feet refused to reach their goal.

After expending lots of nervous energy, I headed for the heavenly smelling clematis, which blanketed the backside of the weather beaten garage. It's gnarled branches, woven intricately through the trellis, never ceased to amaze me. I studied the delicate flowers laden with dewdrops, glistening like living sparkles in the early morning sun. Picking one, I blew on the dewdrops, watching them melt on my fingertips.

The excitement of swinging and beauty of clematis couldn't compare with my vivid memory of the palomino and its rider. I was determined to bug my grandparents!

The back porch screen door suddenly banged shut. With lunch bucket in hand, Grandpa walked down the stairs. Now was my chance!

After taking a deep breath, I dared to ask again, "When can I ride a horse, Grandpa?"

"Enough is enough," he said sternly.

Startled, I stood back.

Grandpa set his black lunch bucket on the ground and picked me up. He set me between two large limbs on the trunk of their plum tree. It stood several feet from the clematis. Without saying a word, he walked to the house and came back with an old belt. After tying it onto the tree he handed me my 'reins'.

"Here now," he said with a wide grin, his curled mustache accentuated at its sides.

"Ride your horse, girl!"

"Thank you! Thank you, Grandpa! But, how will I get down?"

Unbeknownst to me, Grandma was coming out the screen door.

"Veronica?" he yelled, then muttered something in Polish I couldn't understand.

Grandma's flowery print housedress flowed softly as she rushed to the end of the porch. Seeing my predicament, she gave me a huge smile, assuring this was soap making day and would be watching me. I breathed a sigh of relief, excited that Grandpa satisfied my immediate need for a steed!

It started in a plum tree, the feeling of being 'high in the saddle'. I imagined trotting down the road with my horse's flowing mane, brushing my face, just like the boy on the palomino. For now, I was content...

CHAPTER THREE

RACETRACK UNDER WATER

Ellington Hill   February 1951

It was late winter and heavy rains had pelted Ellington Hill for several days. I hopped into the backseat of old Darwin, the family car, thankful for only fog and a light misty rain.

Grandpa John shut the door of the faded black '35 Dodge and slid into the driver's seat.

"It's on its last tires," he said with a sigh.

I stroked the brown velvet seat cover while Grandpa cranked the engine. The soft material felt like Tommy's fur. He was the family mouser and a very friendly cat until Grandpa took out his shotgun. Then he would hide. The shotgun was rarely used, only when a wild animal tried to attack the chickens.

As the motor sputtered, Grandpa hurried back to adjust the choke, his gray felt hat dripping across the top of the seat. My fingers rushed to feel the 'squishy' place, the velvet now flattened and almost black in color.

"Come on Darwin!" encouraged Grandpa. "You're the best car in town and we have to get groceries and take a boat ride to Alex's house."

Grandpa slapped the dashboard and muttered something in Polish, as if Darwin would get the message faster!

I snickered. Sometimes I understood what Grandpa was saying and sometimes not. This time I didn't but kept quiet.

Though Grandpa was proud of his mastery of the English language, he'd often mix in a Polish word or two for my benefit. With eyes slanted toward me, he'd say, "now you can learn the mother tongue, too." The rest of the day, I'd practice the word.

When the car jerked into gear, Grandpa backed out onto the dirt road and we chugged down the hill to town. He turned on the radio but there was so much static it had to be turned off.

His voice suddenly quivered. "People in my country can never afford a car. They are poor and the Communists are getting stronger and stronger. I came by boat from Poland to New York, and then kept moving west to find God's country. We need to always be thankful for everything we have."

When Grandpa said to be thankful for everything, he meant God, Family, America, old Darwin and horses. Not just any horses, but thoroughbreds! "God made them the most beautiful creatures on earth," he would say.

Grandpa's love for race horses started with his brother Alex, who emigrated from Poland in 1910. Uncle Alex and Aunt Julia bought a house across the street from the racetrack. We were headed there now though Grandpa was worried about severe flooding in the valley.

What fun! I thought, as Darwin's windows fogged up. Now I could draw horses on the glass.

I soon noticed Grandpa staring at me through the rear-view mirror.

He finally spoke. "So many days of heavy rain….everyone in town is worried because our two rivers have run their banks by several feet…."

Grandpa's words made little sense to me since I had never seen a flood or at least couldn't remember seeing one.

Changing the subject, I asked, "Grandpa, when will we get to Aunt Julia's and Uncle Alex's?"

He seemed not to hear so I repeated my question.

"Soon enough, Renee," he answered.

"Do we get to see the race horses?"

"Nah….it's still winter and the rains have come and filled the valley like a lake. We'll have to take a boat to get my brother's. I called to make sure he and Julia know we are coming. Last I heard on the radio was a warning to stay away unless you had kinfolk. We'll get groceries then try to get through."

I settled back in my seat.

Mr. Nedd's two-story grocery was an Ellington Hill landmark. The owner and his family lived in the backside of the yellow building.

Mr. Nedd never missed customers because the iron cowbells on the door would wake anybody up!

"Morning, John. How are you and your granddaughter doing today?" asked the tall lanky man with an incredibly thick gray mustache.

I mused because Mr. Nedd never remembered my name. That was all right, though. I never left the store without a piece of candy or gum, compliments of him.

Grandpa gestured with his hands. "We're okay. I mean… not too bad considering the weather. I'm worried about my brother, though. He and Julia are flooded up to the second story. Morning paper says it's one of the worst floods on record, if not the worst!"

"And, aren't you glad you left downtown and moved uphill!" laughed Mr. Nedd.

Grandpa laughed heartily, too.

My Mother said people thought Grandpa was crazy when he and Grandma moved from the valley to Ellington Hill. City folks called it 'the sticks'. With only a thousand dollars, they built a cozy white home on an acre where only a garage stood. That's where they raised a family of three kids, including my mother and her two brothers.

When others moved to 'the sticks' they suddenly needed a school. The townspeople bought the property behind Grandpa's acre and built a kindergarten to eighth grade school. I wanted to go there more than anything, but Mom refused. Such a pity, since there were no green pastures or horses near my city school.

Mr. Ned slammed the cash register shut. "Here's your groceries, John. I do hope everything is well with Alex and Julia. You two be careful and come back soon."

With shopping finished and a cherry tootsie pop melting in my mouth, we drove past Mr. Zinski's gas station. Nearby was a large tract of swamp property that some rich people were trying to buy. Everyone wondered why.

Old Darwin's windshield wipers suddenly quit. Grandpa moved to the side of the road and adjusted them.

"Everything will be okay", he said calmly.

His gray blue eyes met mine. I let out a sigh of relief. If anyone could keep old Darwin running, it was my Grandpa John. Yet one day, I knew he would come home with a new car. That's because Darwin was becoming less and less dependable.

"Son of a gun," said Grandpa with a shrug. "I forgot to pick up the wine at Nick's. We'll have to turn around."

A few Poles, a few Germans, and lots of Italians lived near my grandparents. There was even a family who was Lithuanian, my father's heritage. But Grandpa's best friend, Nick, was Yugoslavian. He was a small man, even shorter than Grandpa, who was five foot three.

Soon, we pulled up to Nick's three story brick house, its big crooked chimney belching huge clouds of smoke.

Old Nick, as everyone referred to him, greeted us at the door. He wore a dark plaid maroon shirt with its sleeves rolled up and a watch on a chain dangling from his pants pocket. His dark skinned hands waved wildly as he talked.

"Come in! Come in! I promised you wine and that I have!" he bellowed.

Old Nick always talked about the 'good life', that it was made for great food and wine. He said that was his reason for making homemade wine and sauerkraut. Grandpa always agreed with him.

"You need to taste my new wine," beckoned Nick.

He led us down the dark narrow stairway to the cellar, a chilly room surrounded by more wine barrels than anyone could imagine. It smelled awful! I was happy, though, for Nick's and Grandpa's enthusiasm.

"Taste this one," encouraged Nick.

"Very good," replied Grandpa.

While they talked and tasted wines, I walked down the rows and fiddled with the spigots on wine barrels or studied the crocks of sauerkraut. Once in a while, a barrel of wine would drip when I turned the spigot. Frantic, I'd turn it off and lick my fingers before Old Nick could see my mischief. The stuff adults liked was disgustingly sour, bitter or both! How could they stand it? I wondered.

My Grandpa was kind of funny. He would tell Nick how great his wine was, then another time he'd spit it out and say it was junk…. after we left old Nick's house!

Armed with a few bottles of wine and several jars of sauerkraut, we drove toward Aunt Julia's. Grandpa's joy spilled over when he began to sing a Polish song. I loved it!

Once in town, Grandpa's voice saddened. "Pretty soon, we will see what the flood is doing to my brother's house and saloon. Training racehorses and running the saloon have been good business for him, even in their troubles."

I wondered if he meant the dead baby when he said 'their troubles'. Once I overheard him and Grandma talk about how Aunt Julia's baby died after it was born. It made them real sad. I wanted to ask questions but was afraid to.

"Look Grandpa, it's like a lake over there, even covering the road," I shouted.

"Now you understand what I was talking about," he said worriedly.

Barriers loomed before us at the intersection of Main and Horton Way. Grandpa stopped Darwin in front of a stern looking policeman and rolled down the window.

"My brother is Alex Keski. I have this letter here from him. He's expecting us," he said to the policeman.

The uniformed man nodded. "Yep, thought I'd seen someone motoring this way. Go ahead, but be careful. The sky's still threatening and it could rain another inch. Be sure you have a jacket for the girl."

"Yes Sir," replied Grandpa.

We carefully made our way past several large orange barrels, finally finding a half dry place to park.

"There's Uncle Alex's boat!" I said excitedly, as Darwin chugged to a halt.

"Don't open the door, Renee! There are holes out there, deep ones, you hear?"

I shook my head.

Grandpa had a sharp, raspy voice when he got mad or was trying to protect his family. It always scared me to do right. I stood up, trying to see the race horse barns but they were too far away.

Alex stabilized the boat, got out and walked toward us.

"Hi Uncle Alex," I said.

Alex, much taller and heavyset than Grandpa, smiled and held up a candy bar.

"Hi there, Renee!" he said.

"You have to get out on my side," cautioned Grandpa.

I slid across the front seat and waited while the men loaded the motorboat with groceries, two jars of Nick's homemade sauerkraut and a couple of bottles of wine.

Uncle Alex helped me onto the boat. He pulled a life jacket out of an old gunnysack, strapped it onto me and sat me in the middle of the boat. I unwrapped my chocolate bar and greedily munched.

The boat swayed heavily when Grandpa stepped in, but eventually steadied. When everyone had their jackets fastened, Uncle Alex started the motor and slowly sped toward his house.

"Hold on!" he called suddenly, turning to avoid a branch that appeared out of nowhere.

"It's probably one of those trees that lined the road to the race track," suggested Grandpa.

"Wow," I said, as we motored past houses with water up to their second floors.

We were soon in the middle of the flooded area. There were no houses, only water on either side. I said nothing. The cold damp air and lone boat in the middle of nowhere felt creepy.

Uncle Alex again slowed to avoid debris and an uprooted tree. I turned and watched the sky behind us grow darker, the fog thicker, and it was only mid-day.

At last, Uncle Alex's faded rustic red house loomed before us. The flood waters had risen to within a couple of feet of the second floor. The house resembled a small southern plantation and was built about 1915. Most curious to me was the first story which was made into a saloon, a gathering place for racehorse people from early spring to fall. Grandpa often went there to talk with his brother. The interior café curtains were tall enough to make it impossible for children to see into the forbidden saloon.

Uncle Alex pointed to the barns at the backstretch of the racetrack. Their roofs were barely visible.

"Would you look at that?" said Grandpa in amazement.

"Yeah, not much that's not under water," replied his brother.

"Can it be saved?" questioned Grandpa.

"If there's any more damage, I don't think so. And my saloon won't make it either.

"When can I go to the races with you, Grandpa? Can we buy a horse?"

"Can't get in till you're eleven years old and we don't have any money for horses. Besides, Grandma thinks it's awful. Your Mom's the only one who'll go to the track with me. There's a beauty about those creatures…."

I understood. The closest I had been to a horse was when I was five, right after the plum tree incident. A man with a pony came to the house and took a picture of me sitting in a western saddle. I loved the photo which Grandma proudly displayed on the dining table. Now that I was eight, I wanted a horse even more!

"There's Julia," pointed my grandfather as she walked out of the house.

Before I could wave, Aunt Julia threw me a kiss.

"Be careful!" she shouted as we pulled up to the stairway.

"We will," called Alex.

The trick was to maneuver the boat so it would be parallel to the stairway. Then it could be secured to the railing without damaging the stairwell.

"You get out first, Renee," commanded Grandpa.

I got off and stepped on the stairway, purposely moving down a step to peek through the saloon window. Excitedly, I was able to see bar stools and supplies stacked on tables in an effort to save them. A few beer steins sat a wall shelf. It looked pretty bleak as the water was several feet deep.

With the boat secured, we greeted Aunt Julia with hugs. Once in the door, a roaring potbelly stove greeted us.

Aunt Julia was always hospitable. She made sure I got lemonade while Alex and Grandpa drank old Nick's wine. They started conversing in Polish then walked to a back bedroom and shut the door.

"Come to the sunroom, Renee," encouraged Julia.

That was all I needed to hear. On the north side of the living room were double doors leading to a glass enclosed veranda. The long narrow room was painted canary yellow. All the furniture, paintings, and plant holders were shades of yellow or yellow prints. There was a magic feeling about the room, always airy and bright even on a dark day like today.

But most exciting of all, the yellow room overlooked the racetrack. Even with only barn roofs showing, I tried imagining what it would be like in the backstretch during race season, to be with horses and jockeys.

Oddly, Aunt Julia never let me stay in the 'yellow' room very long. This day was no exception.

"Come now and sit at the table," she said as she closed the double doors behind us.

Instead, I ran to my favorite chair, a red art noveau classic with clawed hand rests and feet. I spread my fingers between the claws, but they were too small to fit into the imprints. I wondered who thought of making such a chair.

"Would you like some scrambled eggs," asked my aunt as she hurriedly set the table.

Not waiting for my answer, she disappeared into the kitchen.

Mesmerized by the blazing fire in the potbellied stove, I sat contentedly.

In a few minutes, my scrambled eggs were ready.

"What about you? Aren't you going to eat anything?" I asked.

"I have goat's milk and carrot juice. Good for my stomach, you know."

Mom and Grandpa often talked about Aunt Julia being a hypochondriac. They said doctors couldn't find anything wrong with her, even though she complained a lot about her stomach. For me, it didn't matter how weird she ate because I liked her and her food a lot.

As I devoured my eggs, Aunt Julia chatted. "What do you want to be when you grow up, Renee?"

"I don't know, but I want a horse more than anything."

"Well, when you get one, you can bring it here. There's plenty of grass in our backyard."

"Really?" I replied as the bedroom door opened.

Alex and Grandpa came out laughing.

"I'll fix you two some eggs now," offered Julia.

The men nodded and immediately walked to the stove to warm their hands. I realized the bedroom probably wasn't heated.

"It's looking threatening out there again," said Alex. "We best get on our way before it gets too bad."

After the men ate, we got up to leave.

The boat ride back to our car was quiet, a steady rain beginning to fall, the wind picking up.

We said our good byes and climbed into old Darwin just as it started to pour.

Actual newspaper photographs of flood.

CHAPTER FOUR

SWEET SIXTEEN

As the years flew by, so did my obsession with owning a horse. My parents survived by taking me to riding ranches where I could learn the sport. Several babysitting jobs, some for a pittance, paved the way to a dream purchase by my sixteenth birthday. I had managed to save a hundred dollars.

First though, my dad, brother and I had to make a trip to New York. We had to pick up Grandpa John and Mom, who were returning from a trip to Poland. He hadn't seen his brother in 50 years. After Grandma Veronica's sudden death, Grandpa needed the respite.

It was my first time on a plane. As we climbed high above the clouds, lessons in geography and the role of government became clearer. Especially mind-boggling was the realization that a President oversees such a vast land of people and cultures. Those who rule our great democracy have a monumental task.

Ladies and gentlemen, please faster your seat belts as we are approaching LaGuardia International Airport," announced the Captain.

"How was the trip, Mom?" I asked after lots of hugs and kisses.

"Wonderful, dear."

Grandpa John beamed...then turned solemn. "After forty years I was finally able to see my homeland again. We are very fortunate to live in a free country. The KGB followed your Mom and me everywhere, even detaining us one night in Warsaw. I told the authorities that Dr. Antoni was my brother and a Supreme Court judge in the city. After a confirming call, they quickly released us. Don't know what would have happened were it not for my brother."

"Wow," I said, relieved and thankful for their safety.

Grabbing his luggage, Grandpa continued. "One day, Dr. Antoni and his wife drove us to Zakopane, a beautiful mountain resort. They said we could talk freely there. It's such a hard life for those who live in Poland..."

Mom frowned. Then her face beamed. "Meeting my Mother's brother, Marion, was quite an experience.

He answered the door when we knocked but was afraid to let us in, worried there might be repercussions."

"Marisha," he said, "You need to wait at the street curb while I talk to your Father." Dutifully, I waited at the curb.

"We had maybe ten minutes to catch up on forty years," interrupted Grandpa. His sad eyes nearly made me cry.

Mom continued. "I learned that Uncle Marion stayed in Poland while his three sisters traveled separately to America, one being your Grandma Veronica. The women in our family certainly had the pioneer spirit."

"Grandma came across the Atlantic Ocean alone?" I marveled.

"Yes. She told me about crying on the ship because she knew she'd never again see her native land."

I said nothing, touched by this sad revelation.

"And then..." said Mom looking straight at me, "Can you imagine relatives picking us up for dinner in a horse cart? The ride was long and terribly bumpy, a dirt road full of pot holes!"

My eyes widened.

"Renee loves horses," interjected my brother.

I snickered. "Hmm...if people in that city traveled by horse cart, that means they owned at least one horse, lucky them!"

Dad ribbed me as everyone laughed.

After stowing luggage, we crammed into a rental car and headed for the quaint town of Waterford. The schedule included visiting Mom's cousin, Mary, a daughter of one of the three sisters who originally came from Poland.

Adults kibitzed while the teenagers got to know one another, even agreeing to be pen pals. That night, a bottle of vodka was left on the kitchen table. Cousin John snuck it outside and tempted us teenagers to take a swig. I thought I'd die! We knew our parents often downed a shot of whiskey and thought vodka was the same!

Our family time ending, we headed for New York City. A twentieth-floor suite at a landmark hotel on famed Fifth Avenue near Broadway was home for our last two days in the Big Apple.

After a good night's rest, I headed alone downtown. Dressed in a chic suit and high heels, I browsed through stores only seen in magazines. Last on my 'to see' list was the famed Zigfield Follies Theater. Previewing the reader board was incredibly exciting as we had tickets for that night's show.

After four hours of browsing, I knew Mom would be watching for me. Unfortunately, my squished toes were screaming for relief and it was three long blocks to the hotel. After barely a block, excruciating pain signaled the inevitable, removing my high heels, leaving only nylons between me and the dirty sidewalk!

Feeling icky and needy, I eventually succumbed to buying a cheap pair of slippers, if you call anything on Broadway cheap! Once strutting proud as a peacock, I now limped with head bowed, praying no one noticed my feet...

Back at our hotel, I slipped into the bathroom. Underneath the sink were comfy penny loafers. Thank you, God. I almost didn't bring them!

"What happened?" asked Mom.

"Couldn't make it back in my heels," I confessed.

"A little pride, dear?"

"Uh, yes Mom..."

The following day, June 21st, meant a trip to the Empire State Building, a magnificent edifice with an unbelievable amount of offices and so much history behind it. Tired by the end of the day, we all headed back to our hotel.

It was a few minutes before midnight, our last night in glitzy New York, everyone asleep because we were flying home in the morning.

Wide awake, I crept to the window, pulled back the shade and sat on the sill. Fifth Avenue was filled with people, likely returning from the amazing Broadway Follies we enjoyed the previous night. Above the crowd was Old

Ben, shining brightly on the side of an odd shaped building. I watched until its huge hands hit the Roman numeral twelve. Teardrops trickled down my cheeks. No one had wished me a happy sixteenth birthday...

"Wake up, Renee! We need to get to the airport by seven," urged my Mother.

I rolled out of bed, tired, yet anxious to get home. After stuffing mementos into an already overflowing suitcase, I packed crackers, cookies and a candy bar in my carry-on. A last minute throw was those infamous high heels. Never again!!

Our scheduled flight on a Boeing 707 was packed. I begged for the window seat. Grandpa preferred the aisle anyways and Mom was content to sit in the middle. They catnapped while I drooled over cloud formations and studied various terrains. In between times, I filled my diary with flowery descriptions of the trip's treasured moments. By the time we got home, there wasn't an empty page.

"Tomorrow we'll see about your horse," teased my father after we arrived home and emptied suitcases.

"You didn't forget!" I exclaimed.

"Be up early and we'll head out. I told the horse trader we'd be there about nine.

"Yippee!" I yelled, causing Walt to come running through my door.

"Tomorrow I get a horse, Walt!"

"Oh," he said and zipped back to his room.

It was barely sunlight when I woke to the sound of chirping birds. Jeans and a blue t-shirt waited for me after a steaming hot shower. Once dried, I put my thick brown hair in a double ponytail.

"Breakfast is ready," called Dad.

"You excited?" he said as we downed our cereal.

"Am I? It's finally happening, Dad, the thing I've dreamed about since I was five years old."

He wiped his mouth with a napkin. A broad smile came, his blue eyes sparkling like a teenager getting their first car. Maybe, just maybe, he was enjoying this moment as much as I was.

We pulled out of our driveway about eight fifteen. Dad seemed quieter than usual.

"I'm going to buy a horse, too. I can ride or you can have a friend along."

"Are you kidding?" I asked in shock.

My head was spinning. One horse was challenging enough! The thought of caring for two was scary, especially when it was a mile uphill walk to where they'd be pastured. On the other hand, it would be nice to have a friend ride with me as I doubted my workaholic Dad would find the time.

"There it is, Dad, the barn with horses painted all over the front!" My stomach flip-flopped.

"Howdy there...been waiting for you. My name is Sam," said the ranch owner who stood about six feet tall and sported a huge black mustache.

"Pleased to meet you." said my Dad with a handshake. "This is my daughter, Renee."

Sam's squinty blue eyes shifted to me. "Got a couple of horses, a half paint and Tennessee Walker named Pistol, and Danny, a standardbred quarter horse. They're pretty young but I think you might like them. The Walker will pack a smooth ride with his breeding."

I was shocked, knowing from books that Pistol's trot would be considerable less bumpy than other breeds. Never having ridden a Tennessee Walker meant a new adventure.

"I'd like to see them," I replied.

"Sure," said Dad. "Would you believe we had a horse named Danny Boy when I was growing up?"

Sam grinned, then whistled for two young ranch hands to bring the horses. We eyed them and agreed with Sam.

"We'll take both and show me some saddles, too," said my Dad pointing to a tack shop beside the barn.

"Thank you so much, Dad. I didn't expect riding equipment, too!"

My spirit soared as the horses were loaded into Sam's trailer along with the tack.

"Oh daddy, I feel like a little kid again."

After a tender hug, I soaked in my father's love. He reached for a handkerchief and wiped moist eyes.

We said little on the drive to Mr. Johnson's house where the horses would be pastured.

After they were unloaded, Danny Boy and Pistol romped through the large grassy field.

"Looks like they're scoping out their new home," said Mr. Johnson, who quickly came out to greet us. "I'll show you where the feed and other supplies are kept."

"Thanks." I replied.

When Johnson left, we were glued to Pistol and Danny's antics. They surveyed fences, studied stumps, and sniffed the air. Danny neighed and jumped around, squealing after his cohort ran up a mound. The scene was priceless.

"I'll walk home," I said as Dad turned to leave. He saw my bliss and let me be. It was a memorable day for father and daughter, one to cherish.

From that day on, the ritual of school, home to change, then walking to the farm consumed my days. Getting to know each horse's personal quirks and habits was exciting, yet challenging. Once the routine was down, I set myself to emulate my TV idol, the Lone Ranger. Getting Pistol to rear at the top of a small hill on the property like the masked man was my obsession. Though never quite accomplished, I eventually was thankful for any height in rearing.

After nearly two years enjoying equines, less and less time was spent at the ranch. I was getting older and guys and roller skating came to the forefront.

The horses needed to be exercised and guilt was nagging me for not being there. It was time to make a concerted effort to ride. One day I decided to call my friend Connie.

"Can you ride with me tomorrow?" I asked.

"Okay. Sure."

We often rode the power lines but this day chose to cross a two-lane road for more galloping. The ride was uneventful till on our way back.

We were in a slow gallop downhill when Danny got out of control.

"Hold him back," I yelled.

No chance. Her runaway shot ahead, straight for the road.

I held my breath, the scene before me as in slow motion. Danny hit the pavement, slipping and sliding, eventually losing his balance and going down on his left side, on Connie's leg. Thankfully, there were no cars then.

Soon, people in approaching vehicles rushed to get Danny off Connie. Once he was able to stand, someone grabbed the bridle and coaxed him off the road. A good samaritan offered to help get him home, assuring me Danny was shaken but otherwise unhurt.

One broken leg later and a trip to the hospital produced enough anxiety to question having horses. There was already stress associated with them breaking through the pasture fence several times, resulting in my family being called in the middle of the night. Connie's accident and the daily grind got the best of me. It was time to sell.

CHAPTER FIVE

AN OUT OF BODY EXPERIENCE

The kiss of a warm June sun greeted me as I exited the heavy metal doors of my alma mater. Following close behind were a couple of friends and several classmates. We stopped, gazing at the landscape one more time before descending eighty-year-old steps.

Would you believe…?" cried my friend Sheila.

"Can't really," I quipped.

It was our last day of high school, graduation ceremonies a sweet memory, the mood wondrous… until the bus appeared!

I suddenly felt alone… overwhelmed by a sinking feeling—I will never again have to go to school.

The experience was bittersweet, youth cut off to make way for adulthood. If one chose not to pursue higher education, which I was, there would be no more struggles with teachers, homework, classmates, what to wear or what not to wear.

Still, the transition frightened me… until I realized there is a wildness and joy inherent in the daily grind. Life is worth living at any stage. Feeling a little wiser, I climbed on the city bus, ready for my new life.

Barely a week after graduation, financial needs at home turned critical. Vanishing overnight was any hope of attending the State University that had accepted me. Fortunately, a neighbor's connection to a shipyard snared me a file clerk's job, a godsend for my family. A little short of my eighteenth birthday, I was cast into an adult world.

One of the privileges of working at the shipyard was the privilege of attending the christening of a Destroyer. The sonar room was mesmerizing. They had to coax me out!

A daily event for the whole office was waiting for one of our unit secretaries to arrive. She wore a different dress every day. Although reasons abounded as to how she afforded her massive wardrobe, we nevertheless enjoyed the parade!

Within a year, good budgeting bought me an older car, new work clothes and a much-needed washing machine, which greatly pleased my mother. I grew antsy, however, not wanting to be a file clerk the rest of my life. When a local aircraft company advertised for a 'statistical typist,' I tested and got the job.

With one exception, the men in my unit had PhDs and were married. One, on the other hand, was single with a Masters degree. A systems analyst, Rich was smart, gentle and very interested in me. I learned his father died when he was four and his mother never remarried. I marveled that her waitress' salary not only provided a daily living for them but put him through college.

My relationship with Rich blossomed quickly, though discreetly. If we were to marry, company policy would not allow us to work in the same group. I wasn't quite ready for that so our blossoming relationship remained under cover.

During our courtship, my supervisor and his boss were continually goading Rich to pursue his PhD. He always answered, "I have a Masters and that's enough schooling!"

Rich's response puzzled me until an unusual incident settled the issue. For some time, the unit's PhD's had been working on a problem they could not solve. Rich's boss teasingly handed him their material saying, "I'll give it to you since nobody can solve it." Within a few days, he handed back the assignment, problem solved! No one ever approached him again about getting his PhD!

With our family's blessing and delighted co-workers, Rich and I finally married on April 18th, two months before my twenty-first birthday. We moved into a small apartment and went about our daily lives until a surprise pregnancy blessed us with a beautiful daughter. We named her Veronica, after my grandmother. A later genealogy on the matriarchal line revealed that my great-grandmother was also named Veronica, amazing indeed!

Luckily, Dick's pay raises allowed me to be a 'stay at home Mom," a promise I'd made to myself years before, having been a latchkey kid. It didn't take long before we decided that apartment life was too confining. We began looking for a home.

Ironically, my father suggested a new subdivision not far from Ellington Hill, where I had spent my early years with grandparents, a mere four miles from the racetrack. The decision was easy. Living there had been a heart's desire since high school.

Shortly after the move, there was a familiar clip clopping sound. I rushed to the window; amazed to see a horse and rider walking on pavement.

"I can't believe you're walking down this street," I said to the young woman, likely in her early twenties.

"I like to look at the pretty houses," she answered.

"My name is Renee. I had a couple of horses myself," I offered.

"I'm Shelley… just put up a fence to do some jumping. Would you like to come and watch?"

And come I did, the very next day!

Amazingly, Shelley had recently moved her mare to some acreage below our subdivision, a mere block away. The thought of a horse being so accessible made me ecstatic!

"You can ride 'Belle' today," offered Shelley after a couple of visits.

"I'd love to," I replied, anxious to revisit 'bareback heaven.' Shelley didn't even have a saddle!

Belle, a five year old Appaloosa mare, was easy to ride and an excellent jumper. As Shelley rode infrequently, I made a habit of bringing carrots to Belle, often visiting Ethel, the elderly woman who owned the property. When Shelley was on vacation, I was in charge.

Before long, the dream of owning a horse on my own property surfaced with gusto. Ethel's five acres would be perfect if she chose to sell. Now, to convince my better half.

Unfortunately, Rich didn't share my newfound enthusiasm. "You can ride a horse for free at Belle's. Besides, the house is a junker!"

Somewhat discouraged, I involved myself even more with a foreign wives' group I had started. It involved fifty women from different countries, mostly Scandinavians whose husbands came to work for the aircraft company where I had worked. Desperate to learn about American ways, I accompanied them through grocery stores, explaining different products, teaching them about cuts of meat and our variety of vegetables. For Thanksgiving, I suggested traditional pumpkin pie. They balked, finally agreeing to at least taste my pumpkin chiffon pie with gingersnap cookie crust.

"It isn't bad," said the women, still unconvinced pumpkin should be anything but a vegetable!

As winter passed and the last semblance of spring faded, I began to anticipate my birthday. This year June 21st fell on a Sunday. Since the Blue laws were in effect, there was nowhere to celebrate …except the horse races. Happily for me, Rich agreed to go.

"The daily double is my favorite bet," I explained to my husband, who had never been to a horserace.

"Besides," I added, "If we split our money like Grandpa John and I did, we'd have a better chance of winning."

Rich's mathematical mind took over. "Hmm, I'm going to try that."

The morning of my birthday was overcast, a light rain falling. At first I was disappointed, desiring the first day of summer and longest day of the year to be gloriously sunshiny!

By early afternoon, however, a bright sun peeked through long enough to dry the streets. We headed for the track in time to ensure good seats and study the racing form.

"This place is really nice," commented my conservative husband, obviously impressed with the sights and sounds of track life.

Although the thrill of racing stirred my heart once again, it was Rich's winning daily double ticket that cinched our day. My man was hooked! Yes, horses would be in ours lives… if not quite the way I envisioned.

At every racetrack there is a turf club, an elite atmosphere where owners, trainers and avid horse lovers pay a hefty yearly fee for the privilege of being able to have a table, order meals and even bet at private pari-mutuel windows. It is also where track owners and PR personnel entertain VIP's.

Rich's associate at work belonged to the club and convinced us to consider it. "After all," encouraged Sesha, "You two agreed the racetrack was where you wanted to spend your 'fun money,' so why not have all the privileges?"

It took a year before we became Turf Club members. The privilege of having entrance and parking passes was unbelievable. On the other hand, we likely were the poorest club members, sometimes coming with only a couple of dollars to spend! That didn't faze us, though.

It was the sport that drove us, not the gambling. Racing had become our hobby.

As the years passed, we felt Veronica, then five, needed a companion. Being an only child, Rich understood what it was like to grow up without siblings. Unable to conceive and with recurrent pain for the following year and a half, I finally submitted to surgery.

"No matter how diseased your ovaries, I will save a part of one so you can get pregnant," promised my doctor.

Shockingly, the surgery revealed more disease than first thought and demanded removal of both ovaries. In layman's terms, that meant experiencing menopause at twenty-seven years old! The news was traumatic but Rich and I agreed we would adopt.

Within six months, we were blessed with Monica, a beautiful two and a half year old with blond pigtails. Veronica's reaction was amazing.

"I've got something special for you," she said to Monica, promptly climbing the bench of our upright piano. She proceeded to play an original tune for her new sister!

"How do you like that?" she asked.

Monica beamed.

We were floored! Now to find a piano teacher who'd take a five year old!

Life outside horseracing and family life included our church where Rich and I were very active. He was a convert to Catholicism while I was a cradle Catholic. For some time, we had been searching for more spirituality; likely an effect of Vatican II's sweeping changes that left many of the flock feeling like something was missing.

A proposed bible study at our church seemed the likely place to begin our spiritual search. We attended the weekly meetings for a year and a half. During that time, I was puzzled by a man named Joe and a woman named Shari. They talked about miracles and 'knowing God', alien language to me, like I was hearing in a tunnel.

I never had an experience with God and didn't know anyone could besides priests, nuns or the Saints. On the other hand, my husband's comment after his adult baptism was, "It felt like a thousand pound weight lifted off me!" I didn't know what to make of it.

Every week, Joe and Sheri kept inviting the bible study class to 'prayer meetings' at Shari's home. I never considered going until…

One evening while washing dishes, I felt a strange sensation, an impulse to go to that much talked about 'prayer meeting.' I didn't even know what a 'prayer meeting' was? In fact, the term 'prayer meeting' was not in our religious vocabulary! I made up my mind to attend that night, to check out this so-called 'prayer meeting.'

It was a nippy autumn evening, void of moonlight, when I started for Shari's home. The dilapidated one-story house sat far back on acreage, its address numbers all but impossible to read. A string of cars parked on the north side of the property was my clue I was at the right place.

What would be considered a front door was blocked off so I knocked on the weather-beaten back door. No one answered. Eventually, I recalled being told to just walk in.

Inside the dimly lit entry hall were two steps leading to a long hallway, also dimly lit. I thought of turning back, wondering what I was getting myself into?

Finally reaching the lighted kitchen, I heard singing and walked into a tiny dark living room. Several chairs, two sofas, and an old upright piano occupied every bit of wall space. In the middle was a round coffee table with a lit candle. A quick assessment saw about fifteen people, several men and women like me in their twenties or thirties and a few older folks. A fascinating bamboo curtain led to the powder room.

When the song ended, Shari stood up and bear hugged me. Frank, her cohort in the bible study, sat in a deep overstuffed chair across the room.

"Hi, Renee," he said, sporting the widest grin.

"Hi," I said meekly, finding it hard to believe I was in the same environment as the 'miracle' sharers.

After introductions, Shari seated me next to her. During the middle of the next song, a young Asian man walked in and sat there, obviously familiar with the meeting. Everyone in the room seemed happy enough, nothing strange or unusual, though I did not recognize the songs. A couple of faces looked vaguely familiar, perhaps members of my church.

Within a few seconds of 'casing the room' I was suddenly 'caught up' to the ceiling in an out-of-body experience, knowing I was invisible to those below. Tears slid down my face or what felt like my face since my human body was still sitting next to Shari.

"I've been hypnotized," I thought.

The only other option was that it was 'God'. To test my hypothesis, I said, "If that's you, God, then put me down."

Instantly, I came back into my body, sobbing even more than 'up there'!

"I understand," whispered Shari, who gently wrapped her arm around my shoulder.

How could she possibly know what I experienced? Was she some kind of seer?

After the meeting, I was determined to ask. For now, controlling the sobbing and sorting out my 'meeting God' experience was enough to handle.

The meeting finally over, the young man beside me introduced himself, saying. "You'll learn a lot here so we'll be looking forward to seeing you next week."

"Uh, yeah," I stammered, quickly excusing myself to find Shari.

She was waiting for me.

"I didn't know you were experiencing something like that! In fact, I've never heard or read of anyone at a prayer meeting having an out of body experience," she exclaimed in wonderment.

I arrived home that night with holy fear, a thousand questions, and the decision never to go back to 'that meeting.'

Yet, I did go back to that meeting, that house full of people experiencing supernatural things I'd only read in books. Too many questions were answered in the following weeks to justify shirking back. I found my experience to be valid, most likely designed for a needed jolt!

From that point, life took a course unfathomable by me or by my family. As could be expected, Rich's analytical mind and introvert tendencies found the emotionalism of my newfound faith life difficult to accept.

My friends were also poles apart, some saying 'uh?'... the others excited to know more.

Before my out of body experience, scripture meant little to me, certainly not effecting life changes. It took another earthshaking experience to change that.

It was a beautiful morning, clothes needing laundering and mending to do, yet reading the bible seemed more important. I barely got into a New Testament verse when an interior voice said, "You are a Pharisee."

Stunned, I knew God was talking to me, poking holes in my staunch belief that my faith was the only way to God.

Tears flowed.

Discovering that God is sovereign and touches whomever He wills is indeed earth shaking to a triumphal religionist, one intolerant of others' beliefs. Later, I found prayer group members not of our faith were also experiencing a paradigm shift in their thinking. The walls of denominationalism were breaking down.

I still had one big question. Who was this Holy Spirit they talked about at the prayer meetings? I always believed the Father and Jesus were personal while my out-of-body experience focused on God Almighty. Of that I was confident. If asked, my family or anyone in our circle would have said the Holy

Spirit was a 'wind' or 'dove.' The answer to my question came at Shari and Frank's next meeting.

"It's time you received the gift of tongues," pronounced my newfound friend, Bobbi. She didn't even ask my opinion!

"Give Renee the gift of the Holy Spirit, the manifestation of tongues," petitioned Bobbi and several members of the group as they laid hands on me.

Nothing happened.

"Oh well," I said, and went home.

My 'appointment' with this unknown third person of the Trinity came the next day while eating lunch. My tongue suddenly jerked, causing me to spit out my food. The timing was rather strange but I stopped eating, hurried to my bedroom, shut the door and knelt down.

I remembered Shari telling me how she received her 'Pentecostal' experience, so with no other roadmap, I did what she did… push hard to get it, even shout if I had to!

At first, it felt like something wanted to come up out of my innermost being, a place in me I never knew existed. Yet it wouldn't come, like being unable to open a tightly sealed jar. Finally, I shouted out loud, 'working' to manifest whatever was supposed to happen. The result was amazing, like the opening of a dam, an empowerment of love greater than anything I'd ever experienced.

Words in a language I did not know started to come as I yielded my tongue to say them. It was a conscious act, not automatic. I had to consciously speak the words but they definitely weren't of me. Years later, someone told me my tongue was a rare Latin dialect and that I was speaking praises to God. This young man grew up in the Middle East, understanding perfectly what I was saying. That confirmed to me that this 'Holy Spirit' gift was not just jibberish.

With my spiritual release came a 'high' beyond all highs, one that lasted a whole month. People around me, including my questioning husband shook their heads. Even on the rainiest days I would proclaim, "Isn't it a beautiful day?"

At the end of my honeymoon month, I committed a sin. Though not mortal, I was devastated, feeling I let God down after such a dramatic encounter and wonderful experience of love.

My 'blue feelings' lasted until Rich and I attended a special church function with our couples group. A thousand people showed up to hear an eighty-year-old Charismatic priest speak about his experience of Baptism in the Holy Spirit. Before he spoke and while we were singing praise songs, I suddenly heard the audible voice of God say, "I still love you."

Instantly weeping, I was shocked to learn once again that I wasn't entirely my own person, that an entity greater than I had access to my being, all the time. The revelation made an indelible impression, impacting my whole life. That presence was proof that there is a God who knows who we are inside and out. Knowing that insinuates accountability, something we all must address at one time or another in our lives.

Like the Apostle Paul after his conversion, I spent the next three years consumed with a thirst for prayer and spiritual reading material. Questions such as, 'Why was I created?' and, 'What things await one who is chosen of God?' waited for answers.

This internalizing process left me so fulfilled that I quietly slipped out of the racehorse world.

Instead, my passion was sharing the 'Baptism of the Spirit' and getting to know God more. The first candidates were seven women on my bowling team, one of whom was an alcoholic. Others in the group tried to help her but failed. After one week of answering her deepest questions, she experienced a radical conversion. Seeing their friend's change, the other six in our cozy group gradually accepted the message and were filled with God's Holy Spirit. The 'eight' as we were called, had incredible times together and our relationship endures to this day.

After several wonderful years of pursuing the things of God and touching lives, I found myself reading St. John of the Cross and what he called 'the dark night of the soul.' Unbeknownst to me, my dark night was just around the corner.

Great men and women of faith say character, compassion, and strength are sown deep through suffering, not the good times. I eventually realized my valley of travail was actually preparation for the next adventure of my life's journey, an unlikely path were it not for the virtues gained through such difficult times.

CHAPTER SIX

UM, I'M BEING INSPIRED TO BUY A RACEHORSE

The joy of incredible spiritual experiences and a dependable lifestyle was soon smothered by an unending chain of gut-wrenching events.

It began when a close friend, one of the eight in my bowling league, received word her only daughter and grandson had been killed in a truck crash. Soon after that, another in our group lost her son in a terrible biking accident. Another friend lost her thirteen year old after he fell from a scaffolding. The final crushing blow was watching my father survive two heart attacks, only to succumb after the third. Inconsolable grief had stolen my joy.

Not surprisingly, the dark horse of depression found an opening in my once perceived impenetrable soul. Grief surrounded me like a monster, throwing its darts of accusations such as "where is your God now?"

Seemingly endless funerals curtailed spiritual meetings. The once exciting world of horseracing became a dim memory. Our families ached for the deceased and those left behind.

My sole link to personal sanity was my bowling league... until I heard a 'still small voice' say "Give that up." Ego was about to be impaled on the cross.

Shocked beyond belief, I said aloud, "Now there's nothing left just for me!"

After the initial shock of losing my last pillar of normalcy, I managed to have an upbeat attitude for a few months. Yes, the sport was missed, but there's light at the end of every tunnel. I would just wait for mine.

Disappointed after several months with no hint of light, Rich suggested a shopping spree at the mall. We passed Century Downs, which I usually avoided looking at. Instead, a quick glance resurrected sweet memories, the thrill of watching God's creatures race toward the finish line. The experience was surreal... hazy mist hovering above the tote board... center field's glistening lake.... two horses dueling down the home stretch on their morning workout. Crowning the 'perfect' scene was my 'ice cream cone' mountain, gleaming magnificently beyond the green valley.

Resentment rose its ugly head.

Why had I been deprived of the things that meant so much for so many years? At least the race trackers were having fun! The rest of the 'eight' were still bowling and here I was...taken out of everything!

Yes, my personal demons were having their heyday. That's when mystics say you see your true self, unable to hide imperfections, where 'why me ism' smothers virtue, light, and faith.

Even mall shopping couldn't get me out of my funk. I thought of Delores, my dear friend who suddenly was inspired to buy a pony, the last person I could imagine doing that. She was into dogs, didn't even like the equine species! One day, her family upped and moved into a home on acreage where Arabian horses, especially studs, became their focus. I tried not to be jealous, eventually deciding to be happy for my friend. That change of heart likely prepared me for a divine encounter that would soon shatter my darkness.

It happened while driving home one late afternoon from Delores' ranch. I had just passed the thoroughbred farm of a well-known trainer, an old-timer Grandpa John often mentioned. My thoughts weren't particularly taking me anywhere when an inspiration strong as a boom box invaded my mind...

"Buy a racehorse, Name him 'For His Glory', and Run in My name."

The overwhelming voice shocked me. With the penetrating words came a sensing the horse should be a two-year-old. I had never been to a racehorse ranch nor did I know anyone close to me who had. Uncle Alex and Julia died before I got married so there was no longer anyone in the family with a tie to racing.

My mind reeled. How do you purchase a racehorse?

Adding to the weight of this calling was wondering how my husband would respond. At that time I was involved in two churches. The Catholic one had no qualms about racing but my involvement with a Restoration church might be a problem. Surely, a racetrack to them conjured up ominous overtones of sin, vice, and of course, gambling. Restoration theology taught about supernatural gifts and what it takes to walk like manifested sons of God. Wouldn't they see that I had a call on my life to do just what they were teaching?

More important was confronting Rich about my 'inspiration'. After all, he was a brilliant mathematician and logic reigns with the left brained. On the other hand, his conversion included 'feeling' like a thousand pound weight lifted off when he was water baptized.

Rich balked as I nervously tripped through my story.

"How much will it cost? We only have seventeen hundred dollars in savings. Would that buy a decent horse?" he questioned.

Exhausted from explaining, I realized my comfortable life with few challenges was over. Maybe a dark night of the soul was not so bad after all!

Yet, inside me was a great stirring, an excitement unparalleled. What greater thing can a person know than why he or she was created, that they were chosen for a *Divine destiny*. That realization is impossible to verbalize. The scene was set and I had been cast for 'Act One.'

It took a nail-biting week before Rich's answer came. "Okay. If you can find a thoroughbred for the money we have, go ahead."

I melted and rushed into his arms.

Following my instincts the next morning, I drove to the ranch I'd passed by so many times, where the inspiration to buy a horse named 'For His Glory' came. It's narrow driveway led past a small white picket fenced home, then circled around to a large ramshackle barn. Beyond the barn stretched a quarter mile oval training track, its fences weather beaten and leaning at a severe angle. Although the facility looked ancient, I knew it housed a wealth of horseflesh.

A few deep breaths gave enough courage to stop and get out of the car. Surprisingly, a nice looking man in his early thirties quickly walked toward me.

"Can I help you?" he said warmly.

Stammering, I replied… "Um, yes. I'm being inspired to buy a racehorse!"

The man's gentleness and understanding attitude took me by surprise. He was clean cut and his lean frame reminded me of a well known jockey.

"I'm Myron Lowe," he said extending his hand. My knees knocked at the realization this was the jockey!

"Let me take you around and show you some of our horses. We have a nice filly for sale for $7,000."

Nearly choking, I wondered how in the world we could buy a racehorse with our meager savings.

"Don't think we can manage that," I said hesitantly.

"Well, we'll come up with something. Follow me."

The odor of fresh hay and straw permeated the barn air as workers scurried around us. A whiff of manure from a cart hastily wheeled away by a farm worker was, uh, strong.

Reminiscent of the Wild West, I was entering a scene, excited about becoming part of an adventure.

"That's Tyler and there's Camille," said Myron pointing down the shed row. "Tyler's been here forever and Camille's just learning about cleaning stalls and working around horses. She's a natural
and the horses already love her."

I said nothing, taking it all in.

The interior of the barn had wide aisles but an unbelievably low ceiling. A horse tall as Glory would have to duck in order for his ears not to rub against the ceiling.

"That's "Super Sue," pointed Myron. She's a beauty and will be broken after the first of January. Even for $7,000 she's a good buy."

I studied the bay yearling with a white diamond marking on her forehead. She looked comfortable in the twelve by twelve space bedded by several layers of straw. Black and green buckets were attached at either end of the stall, one for water, and the other for grain. Iron bars fronted Super Sue's and most of the nicer stalls, reminding me of a prison. Myron read my mind.

"Horses like to chew on wood so these bars work well. In fact, horses love to eat wood. We creosote at least the top portions of fences to resist the cravings of these four-legged creatures. I have watched one gnaw off a large jagged piece of wood and swallow it. Makes me cringe to this day!"

I was all ears, drinking in every word, musing about my years with Pistol and Danny Boy.

We walked toward a stall where a large chestnut recognized Byron and let out a short whinny.

"This is Chico G, an older gelding-that just keeps running. Always seems to bring in a paycheck."

I rubbed the gelding where horses loved to be rubbed, behind their ears. The rush was unexplainable.

I suddenly thought of Grandpa John, who died a couple of years before. No one would be thrilled more about my vision than he. We were racehorse lovers, Grandpa and I. My parents cared little about equines but enjoyed racing. Even before we were old enough to get into the track, they brought Walt and me along and parked next to the track fence. That way we could stand on the car roof and watch the stretch runs.

"Let me talk to Jake, the owner of this place," suggested Myron as I entertained my nostalgia.

He was soon back with Jake, the trainer I had often seen in the winners circle. He was a rough looking man, about six feet tall, and walked with a limp. His wavy black disheveled hair and mustache reminded me of a bad cowboy in a John Wayne movie.

"Nice to meet you," I said nervously.

Jake's deep-set eyes commanded attention and his sharp booming voice made me feel somewhat uneasy.

"I hear you're interested…uh… inspired to buy a horse. Well, I'm sure we can help you... so follow me."

We passed the barn area and headed toward two large pastures. I stopped, catching a quick glimpse of a tiny white house, probably a studio with bath behind. Its crooked chimney belched thick gray smoke that drifted sideways in the morning breeze.

Jake turned and offered, "My best ranch hand, Little John, has lived there for forty years. I'm sure you'll meet him."

We walked through a patch of tall green grass then stepped between two cross fences separating a couple of pastures. Jake proudly pointed to some of his stock and said he owned over twenty acres.

"There he is." pointed Myron.

At the end of a field was a large bay gelding. He looked strong, though bony and rather ugly. His large head and roman nose coupled with an extremely long coat of winter fur was not my idea of a racehorse. A white marking on his forehead seemed the only redeeming quality.

"He's just come off the range east of the mountains. That's why he looks like that," explained Jake.

"We own him (pointing to Myron) and you can have half interest for $1700. That way you only pay half the bill."

I stared quite a while at the grazing animal. Shaggy or not, I knew this horse was destined to be mine. Now, to get Rich's okay...

Jake reminisced as we walked back to his house. "I've broken so many horses...can't remember the number. Can't do it anymore cause this sixty plus year old body won't take it."

"Wow," I've got thrown a couple of times but nothing compared to you."

Jake didn't respond, obviously realizing I had some experience with horses.

"This is my wife, Deenie," said Jake as she greeted us on the porch.

"Nice to meet you," I said to the frail gray haired woman who sported a knitting needle in her bun.

Jake waved us through a small living room with matching brown leather lounge chairs and a TV. Beyond was a roomy kitchen with a large oak table covered with a red tablecloth. Deenie poured coffee for the three of us and disappeared into the living room. I sat across from Jake and Myron, mentally preparing my words.

"Four things are necessary for this purchase," I said with unusual confidence. "One, the horse would have to be a two year old, which he will be. Second, he would have to be renamed 'For His Glory.' Third, I can choose the stable colors. And four, I would be able to pick the stable name."

Jake looked at Myron, agreeing they were all possible, though I might have to wait a while for the stable name.

"This is dependent on my husband's approval, you know?"

"Sure, take your time. We'll be here," snickered Jake.

Riding home on cloud nine, I braced for my husband's response. Spending everything we had in savings was pushing the envelope and I knew it. Yet, this racehorse thing was a true inspiration from God. I would have bet my life on it.

"What a scrumptious dinner!" said Rich that evening. "How did things go on your trip?"

"Honey, I think I've found the horse."

As expected, his eyelids lifted and soft brown eyes widened. "Well, how much will it cost?"

Quoting the $1700 figure, my man quickly saw the depletion of our life savings, recently inherited when his mother died suddenly.

"I'll think about it," he said and walked upstairs to the den. The door shut.

His decision would be a leap of faith for any husband, requiring internal fortitude to believe your wife, that she really had this revelation from God. I had total confidence that everything would work out. Of this I was sure.

My mind raced that night, realizing the purchase price was but a drop in the bucket to the task of preparing a horse to race. There was a monthly cost to train, shoe, vet bills, race entry fees, etc. Thankfully, this was not my vision. Peace came and I slept like a baby.

CHAPTER SEVEN

FOR HIS GLORY

Golden sunlight barely dusted the horizon when I slipped downstairs and plugged in the coffee pot. After it's last sizzle, I heard Rich's alarm go off. Routinely, he would shower, dress, eat cold cereal and drink a cup of java before leaving for work. Filled with anticipation, I sipped my coffee.

"After work, I'll go with you to Jake's," said Rich as he reached for a mug.

"Oh honey, thank you, thank you!" I said, smothering him with hugs and kisses.

"Uh huh," he smiled back.

My insistence on bacon and eggs instead of cereal sent him out the door humming.

At five thirty sharp, we pulled into Jake's driveway. He and Myron were watching his wife, Deenie, putter with purple mums that filled a wooden tub on the front porch.

Myron welcomed us. "The bay is tied up but he's pretty skittish. It's better you don't do much with him yet. It appears the farm he came from did little if any work on him."

The jockey's words floated through the air. I heard but was already mentally preparing to be a racehorse owner, or at least half a one.

"What do you think, Rich?" asked Jake.

"Give me the particulars about costs of breaking and training," my husband replied in a definite business mode.

Jake crooked his neck and gestured. "We'll split costs. But since we have a vested interest, we'll throw in a few extras. How does that sound? Oh, I forgot to tell you. If we pay a registration fee of $500, the yearling qualifies for the two year old championship at the end of racing season."
Rich thought for a second, then looked at me.

"Okay, we'll go for it," I said.

From that moment, we trusted Jake and Myron to educate us in racehorse ownership. Being 'green' in the industry, we listened and believed everything they said. Within a few days, the necessary papers were signed with a check for $1,700 and a promissory note for $500. The word God had given me was on its way to manifestation.

Trips to the farm became commonplace. One late Monday morning, I drove up to the now familiar white house and knocked on the door. Neither Jake nor Deenie answered. Thinking someone might be in the barn area, I went there. No luck. Even the help had left. Not sure what to do, I climbed on the first crossbeam of a fence overlooking Jake's property. Our baby was grazing at the furthermost end of the north pasture. I could barely see him.

Pondering the scenario, I wondered why God wanted anything to do with racehorses? The answer came clear as a bell...

"These are MY horses. I bring them to their highest potential as I bring YOU to your highest potential. And I use these people whether they believe in Me or not to bring MY horses to their fullest potential."

The Creator of the Universe had just unveiled a mystery. Never again would I question why I was sent to the racehorse world. There was a Divine purpose at Jake's and at the track. All that was required of me was to relax and let the story unfold. I needn't struggle to make things happen. That kind of knowledge cannot be bought. It is half the battle of walking in vision. If you know that you know that you know something, it is much easier to trust and go with the flow. This revelation helped me surrender even more to God's full purpose and will for my life.

"How're you doing there young lady?"

Caught off guard, I turned around and blurted, "Now I really know why I'm here."

Jake stared at the ground as the revelation was shared. When he did look up, his dark eyes became animated.

"I believe in God because I was an alcoholic till five years ago...used to go to AA. It helped me get through the process. I don't go anymore because I conquered my addiction. I'll never touch a drink again."

"Hey there," interrupted Myron. "How are you doing today?"

"Great," I replied, disappointed because Jake had opened up to me. I wanted to hear more.

Myron took a cue from Jake and addressed me. "I thought we'd talk about breaking the bay."

"Sounds good," I answered.

As Jake waved me back to the house, I pondered his words, marveling that he had been delivered of his addiction.

Deenie, walking with a noticeable limp, had coffee and cookies waiting at the table. Jake took a sip and passed me an envelope. "This here is your paper officially naming your horse *For His Glory*."

Overcome with emotion, I was unable to hold back the tears.

Jake managed a half grin and fiddled with his coffee cup. Myron's gentle brown eyes met mine. He understood my God talk, having acknowledged a few days earlier that he was a believer.

After a couple of quiet minutes, Deenie refilled her husband's cup. He mumbled a 'thanks' and began to share when Rich arrived. He had taken off work early.

"I was just telling your wife," Said Jake, "that every thoroughbred yearling is considered a two year old on January first, regardless of when they were born. Most horses are born between February and July. For His Glory was born in April. That means he will be broken before he is even two years old. The later a horse is born, the later it may have to wait to race as a two year old. Horses mature at different levels. They must pass certain tests to endure a grueling race. Be patient and you'll see Glory run soon enough. In fact, since he's the biggest boned thoroughbred I've ever seen, I'll bet we can start off the racing season early on."

"Sounds good to me," commented my husband.

"That would be something," I added.

Like a newbie, I was hungry for any information about thoroughbreds. But for now, my brain was on overload. So many wonderful things happened so fast. After a heartfelt "thank you," we headed home with For His Glory's papers in hand.

After that day I visited Jake's ranch and watched 'Glory' graze as much as possible. The days turned into weeks and the weeks into months.

Mid November I recognized a groom named Jennifer was paying more than ordinary attention to Glory. Turns out Jake and Myron sold a quarter of their interest to Jennifer and her family. My desire to someday own all of Glory now seemed totally out of reach. Yes, indeed. Jake was a horse trader. I wondered what other 'surprises' awaited me in this faith venture. Though Jake assured us there would be no more surprises, this was a precursor to many trials that line the path of one's vision.

Come January, it was time to break old Glory, Jake's now common name for him. I didn't care for that designation. Everyone else just called him Glory.

Shaggier than a bear and with his roman nose bigger than ever, he was brought into the barn to begin the process of learning to relax when hands or bodies needed to work with him.

One particular day will stand forever in my mind. I arrived to see Jennifer standing in front of Glory's stall. She was barely five feet tall and at almost 16.3 hands he towered over her.

Glory's hindquarters were pushed right against the door opening and he wasn't budging! She tried to get him to move, but with no luck.

Suddenly Jake appeared, yelling obscenities at Jennifer and the horse. With dashing bravado, he strode toward a wall where a long chain with huge links hung. Yanking it off the hook, he walked back to the stall door, moved Jennifer out of the way, and opened the door. With all his might he smashed the chain on Glory's hindquarters.

We stood there flabbergasted, in awe of the trainer's knowledge and authority. Glory practically flew to the other side of the stall and stood quietly facing us.

"Whoa son. It's okay," Jake said repeatedly, almost singing the words.

He calmly walked out of the stall and started in again, shouting at Jennifer, "You don't let a horse get away that long with anything! Besides, you're too short to halter horses and handle them!"

Poor Jennifer's days were limited from that point. In less than a year she left Jake's, had a baby daughter, and was working at another profession.

Her love for Glory never waned, however, as she often came with her family to watch his progress.

By March, Glory was broken to saddle. Now, a couple of challenges arose for me. All trainers and stables have their own jockey silks available to new owners without cost. Silks are not cheap, yet I began pushing for custom ones that would reflect my mission. Confronting Rich and Jennifer's family was not a thrilling prospect. However, an incredible experience proved to be the needed impetus for both to agree.

It happened one afternoon when our oldest daughter, Veronica, came running into the house.

"Mom! Come see the rainbow!"

I couldn't leave that second so she called for Monica and they ran out the front door. Having a rainbow as a design on the jockey silks had entered my mind. Was this a sign?

"Mama! Mama! Come see," the girls shouted as they burst through the door. "There's a dove flying around the rainbow."

Stunned, I ran out. Unfortunately, the rainbow, which was positioned right in front of our house, had all but disappeared and no dove was to be seen.

"But we saw it!" voiced the girls.

From that moment I knew the design of For His Glory's silks would be Kelly green with a rainbow and dove underneath. They were signs of the Old and New Testament. The rainbow was a sign that God would never again flood the whole earth. The dove symbolized Jesus' promise to send the Holy Spirit.

I needlessly worried since my husband and Jennifer's family had no problem with the silks or the extra expense. They even thought the process would be exciting.

The second challenge involved pushing a new stable name. I anticipated some flack since the present one (given automatically by the trainer at purchase) included each of the owner's surnames. I knew the stable name should be 'Revelation Six Two Stable.'

"And I looked, and behold, a white horse. He who sat upon him had a bow; and a crown was given to him, and he went out conquering and to conquer."

Rev 6.2

Switching to such a blatantly religious name might not set so well with non-religious people. That didn't pose a problem either though it would take a year to establish.

As time passed, I realized there are thorns beneath every rose. Though many race trackers are good hardworking people, I began to see a less appealing side of the business. Putting the animal above everything, even the Creator, was widespread. There was the never-ending struggle to make money, often to the detriment of horses, owners, and jockeys. Owners can be inordinately demanding, their criticism sometimes valid, other times not. And of course, there are mean people who abuse their animals or their help. Racing is one of the most grueling professions. Trainers and their help work at least six days a week and often seven. Only the hardiest survive.

The thorn beneath my rose surfaced when Jake's once gracious attitude suddenly became guarded. His domineering nature brought me to the point I was afraid to even touch Glory. He enjoyed wielding his power though I realized there's always the fear that an owner could be injured because of inexperience. Just because one has been around riding horses does not necessarily prepare you for the moods of a racehorse. They can turn faces very quickly and racehorse people have scars to prove it.

Glory, though gentle in the stall, was difficult to manage. He was very high-strung, making him skittish at the least provocation. Saddling the equine was a major fete and soon there was a scuffle to see who would not be his groom.

I realized Jake was curious as to what kind of strange woman he had on his hands and what future lie for this lowly horse named For His Glory. My focus, however, was not on having a Kentucky Derby winner but to show God's love to race trackers. After all, how many horse people were interested in God at all or even went to church? Almost none, I thought. Unbeknownst to me, other kindred spirits were also working quietly in the backstretch with a similar mission. Our purpose was clear. Race trackers weren't going to church so we were bringing the church to them!

My Pastor blessing Glory.

An unforgettable moment of Glory gently lifting up Marnie's 3 yr. old daughter

CHAPTER EIGHT

FIRST RACE JITTERS

Seasonal rains lessened as April breathed its last hoorah. Left behind were rampant wildflowers and trees bulging with new growth after an especially late winter. Marveling at God's handiwork, I drove to the track, hoping to catch Glory before his morning gallop.

Unfortunately, he was already on the walker. Jake stood nearby, his eyes fixed on Glory.

"I'm entering him in the third race on opening day," he said.

"Opening day?" I replied in astonishment. "That's only a week away?"

"Yes, opening day," he repeated, trying not to crack a smile.

"Wow!"

I probably shouldn't have been surprised. Jake mentioned months before he'd like to run Glory early. I just didn't think that early.

"I'll work your horse two days before the race. You might want to be here," he suggested.
"Let me know what time," I said, grinning ear to ear.

Opening day at any rack is charged with energy and one of the most attended of the meet. Trainers must submit their entries two days before the proposed race. Working your horse two days prior is a given. However, you won't know whether your horse made the draw until later that same morning, after workouts. There is an obvious letdown when you don't make the card. Less ominous is ending up on the also eligible list. That's no guarantee, either. If no horses are withdrawn the morning of the race, you're automatically scratched!

"What if...?" I questioned Jake.

"Don't worry about getting in the race," he assured. "Two-year-olds have an advantage since most of them aren't ready or approved this early in the season."

I breathed a sigh of relief...still praying Glory would make it on the first toss.

Jake walked to the other side of the barn. "Get Glory off that walker!" he called to Jay, one of his new hands.

Jay hurried past me to get a shank. "How are you doing, Renee?"

"Fine," I replied.

I followed as Jay led Glory to his freshly cleaned stall. He checked his water and oats, talking to him as he worked.

A tinge of jealousy surfaced. If only I had my own place...then I could have that kind of relationship with Glory.

"You must be excited about the possibility of running opening day?" queried Jay.

"On pins and needles," I replied, my conscience growing edgier by the minute.

Convicted, I scolded myself for coveting Jay's relationship with my horse. I didn't have his unique gift and never would. Forgive me, Lord and help me be satisfied with ownership. You've given each of us a role in bringing Your horses to their fullest potential.

"Glory's on the muscle. Darryl, our exercise boy, can hardly hold him back," continued Jay.

"That's exciting," I said.

"Have a good day," waved Jay as he ran to wash down another horse.

"You, too," I said sheepishly.

A rustling sound turned my attention back to Glory. He was circling his stall, searching for the ideal place to plop. Down he went, his legs flailing, his right hoof banging the wall. Being such a large horse, there's always a fear of being cast, of being cornered against a wall, unable to get up. If not freed, a horse can die and some have.

His itch finally relieved, he jumped up, shook off the loose straw, and eyed me.

"Hey, big horse, do you realize you're going to race in a week?"

His big black eyes sparkled.

"You do know," I chuckled.

His head suddenly smacked across mine, knocking me off balance.

"Whoa there, big horse!" I said sternly.

His eyes softened.

"I have to go now. You stay healthy, you hear? "

Ignoring me, he drank from his water bucket.

I walked away...then turned back. "Don't forget Glory; I've been waiting for this a long time."

His head popped up, chin slavering, a very funny sight!

He watched me walk away to make my call to Rich.

'Hi honey. Guess what?"

"I'll call our partners and let them know," said Rich excitedly.

"Can you believe our hopes and dreams are finally materializing," I raved.

Rich hesitated. "It's our horse's debut..."

"I can hardly wait!" I answered.

"Me too."

The day of the workout was dry but overcast. A weather front was moving in and the rains were expected to hit Thursday, opening day. That was a concern for all.

'Everyone's here," I remarked to Rich after parking in the backstretch lot and seeing our partner's vehicles.

"We're early. But they're really early!" joked my husband.

Jake greeted us at the foot of the guinea stand (a platform where people gather to watch workouts). We joined the group, which huddled in front of the railing, a few feet from horses coming onto the track. Jake's hands clung tightly to the cyclone fence.

"Here he comes!" exclaimed Jerry, a friend of ours from church whom we'd found also had an interest in a horse. "I came to support you."

"Thanks," echoed our group. We were continually surprised at the great camaraderie of horse owners.

"I'm nervous,' I whispered in Rich's ear.

"It'll be okay," he assured me.

Like a bunch of Cheshire cats, we whispered encouragement as Glory stepped onto the track, wondering how fast he would run the four furlongs. Handicappers would note all his works but pay special attention to the most recent. Ah...to see our horse's name in print!

Darryl, now an apprentice jockey, trotted Glory to the six and a half furlong pole. He turned and galloped him down the stretch, several feet from the guardrail. At the quarter mile pole, he drove the big horse into the rail and let him go. He raced easily, closing well at the finish line.

"The time's real respectable,' encouraged Jake after checking with the track's official timer.

"I wonder if he black lettered?" suggested my husband.

All of us agreed the time was fast. Black lettering means running the fastest time that day for the distance and is highlighted in racing forms.

"Now we just wait," said Jake as he limped toward the barn, his arthritis acting up.

With two hours to kill, we hit the track cafeteria where the buzz of race patrons and aroma of sizzling bacon greeted us. Familiar faces wished us luck as we waited for seats. Word had already gotten around!

With full stomachs and anticipation sky-high, we headed for the racing office. This was the group's first opportunity to see where major racing decisions are made. I recognized several trainers or their representatives, everyone hoping their entries would make the cut.

The room suddenly quieted when the racing secretary walked in. He held up what looked like a Plexiglas shaker, similar to those used for lotteries. After it spun, one ping-pong ball was retrieved at a time. Each ball had a number and horse's name. Number three popped up first, then five and eight.

"Number seven, For His Glory," called the official.

"He made it!" we all cried out.

I turned to see Jake standing in the doorway. He cracked a smile and took off for the barn, his mood considerably better than usual.

It was a quiet ride home. Barring unforeseen circumstances, Rich and I knew the fruit of months of hard work and significant financial investment was finally within reach.

"You mean Glory's going to run opening day?" exclaimed Monica.

"That's right," piped her Dad.

"Oh no! We can't go because it's during school?" voiced Veronica.

"Darn," moaned Monica.

"Maybe next time," encouraged Rich.

After dinner, we hotfooted to our neighborhood drug store to buy a racing form. The clerk grinned wide and whispered, "I'll watch for your horse because I'm taking opening day off!" We knew a lot of workers were doing the same as there's more pomp and pageantry after the long winter.

Before reaching the car, I had scanned the form's front page, and then turned to the third race.

"Look where they've pegged him!" I said unbelievingly.

"At the bottom? replied Rich.

"And only one other horse black lettered!" I contended.

"Who cares?" We both finally agreed.

It didn't really matter where handicappers pigeonholed us. We just wanted the thrill of seeing our horse run...and come out safely! On the other hand, the number seven is significant as it is used 54 times in the book of Revelation alone. Many times it tells of God's creative work. It is the number of completeness and perfection, both in the natural and spiritual. We would wear number 7 proudly!

Opening day at Century Downs finally arrived. Instead of May sunshine, black clouds on the western horizon threatened rain. Track personnel crossed their fingers as large crowds meant too little room under cover.

Dressed in our finest, we left for the racetrack two hours early. Even then, Rich had to contend with heavy traffic.

"Owner parking is awesome!" quipped Rich.

"Yep," I agreed. "No more mile hikes or tired legs after a long race day."

We gawked at television trucks and VIP parking outside the clubhouse, finally having the thrill of presenting our passes at the owner/trainer window. Lines were minimal, and admittedly, we felt special.

Once inside, the air was electric. A well known news anchor was interviewing a prominent trainer and city official. Fans waited eagerly for a local boxing celebrity who was to crown the winner of the feature race.

"They're absolutely gorgeous!" I remarked of the pink and white geranium baskets hanging several places in the clubhouse and grandstands. Rich nodded.

Most stunning was the racetrack infield. It was covered with myriad multi-colored perennials, the work of numerous college students. Past the clubhouse was the mouthwatering aroma of sizzling hotdogs and fresh beer wafting in the air. Only the blowing of the bugle and excitement of horses parading to the post were needed to complete the pageantry.

Rich and I found it all but impossible to focus on the first two races. When they ended, we grabbed our identification badges and entered the paddock where Glory and the other entrants would be saddled. The atmosphere was surreal.

Nostalgia gripped me...I was twelve years old...standing with Grandpa John outside this same paddock, Grandpa casing the horses, waiting for a hunch, and many times he got one.

Through an incredible series of events, I was now standing inside the paddock, sharing the exhilaration of the sport of kings. Tears fell for the privilege. Oh Grandpa, how I wish you could be here today...

"Here they come!" called Jennifer and her family.

I shook as the third race entries walked into the paddock in numerical order. Jay was leading Glory, who looked fit but incredibly nervous.

When Jake joined us, I shared my concern.

"...Just exceptionally high strung," he accentuated.

I turned my attention to Glory's braided mane and tail. Thanks to Jay and his wife Janice's efforts, they were woven with blue and white pom-poms. Grandpa John would be delighted as he had luck betting on decorated horses.

"Glory looks and feels great," said Janice as she joined us.

We beamed.

"Does he have a chance?" I whispered.

Janice flipped aside her long bangs and wiped her eyes. "Hard to tell. There're just babies. You do the best you can to get them ready. Glory's fit and loves to run. He is a sweetheart to work with on the ground...but get someone on him and watch out! He's a ball of lightning, tough to ride."

I chewed on that response.

As grooms brought their starters out of the stalls, number six, a stocky black gelding (a male horse often gelded to make him better-behaved and easier to control) acted up. I grimaced because Glory was close to its heels. The adept handler quickly got control by securing the lead chain over the gelding's nose.

I chewed a fingernail, very aware that two-year-olds tend to be skitsy, flying off the handle in an instant. Your horse may not originate trouble but follow with copycat acts.

"Glory was unnerved by that black gelding," commented Rich.

I watched Jay dig his heels into the dirt to keep Glory from blowing up.

"This is nerve-racking," I said aloud.

"I'm with you!" echoed Jennifer with a weak smile.

"Do your stuff, Glory!" encouraged Rich as he passed us.

But Glory wasn't paying attention. He recognized the racetrack beyond the paddock hedge. Like a stallion sniffing the dessert wind, his proud head hunched and then stiffened. Stopping abruptly, he stared at the lit up tote board. I could almost hear him thinking...

'There's the home stretch...where my mane flies high in the wind...where I'm asked to run fast as I can...where the snapping of the whip pounds my hindquarters or taps strongly on my shoulders...where my rider asks for more and more...everything I can give...where he and I become one. That's why I was created...to sail with the wind...for His glory!

"Ohhh." gasped the crowd both inside and outside the paddock.

Two horses in front of Glory suddenly freaked, jumping around wildly. Their handlers struggled to turn them in circles, the most effective way to curb mischief and calm hot-blooded horseflesh.

Those behind the culprits were forced to slow down or stop a second time, hard for any group of horses, let alone two-year-olds.

My eyes shot back to Glory. Thankfully, the fracas had diverted his attention. He backed up and pranced around, his neck covered with white lather.

Panic struck me. What if he got injured, or fell, or broke a leg? Injuries can sideline a horse for weeks or even the whole season. A broken leg meant death!

Jake read my mind. "He'll be fine. You'll get used to it. They're just (expletive) two-year-olds."

Jake was right. Things would work out. Otherwise, why had I been called to this mission field?

The chaos ended as quickly as it started. Each of the horses went into their stalls to be saddled. Glory hesitated then shot into the stall.

It takes a team of four or five to bridle, saddle and certify a horse before they are allowed to step foot onto the track. An agent from the horse racing commission must open each horse's mouth and check their upper lip for an identification number. The tattoo must match their formal registration number.

It was Glory's turn to be checked. He balked on the official's first try, and then submitted. The agent noted something on his clipboard and left. We were okay for now.

Saddling was another matter. Like most horses, Glory resisted the last couple of buckles that secured the saddle, necessary for the safety of the jockey. He made his presence felt, prancing sideways, eyes darting between humans and the unfamiliar environment of a noisy crowd. An attention getter, he kicked hard at the backboard. Though not uncommon, kicking is definitely discouraged as shoes can be loosened, even thrown.

By now, my knees were knocking. Working with high-strung thoroughbreds in such a confined area is risky and I'd seen people hurt.

God, please don't let Glory or any of our help be one of those statistics! I begged. Luckily, we weren't the only horse acting up. The stocky black horse in the number one stall was giving his help a rough time. Watching their struggle somewhat eased my tension.

Once saddled, the jockey room door opened and they walked toward us. I was immediately drawn to the various silks and their emblems. Most represented the trainer's stable though one bright yellow silk was custom made. I dreamed of the day Glory had designer silks with our own logo. For now, I had to be content with Jake's drab faded ones which displayed little originality, only his initials.

"Look's like Glory's feeling pretty good today," quipped Darryl as he approached us and shook hands.

We all nodded and wished him a good race.

Darryl was tall for an apprentice jockey, close to six feet. Although his good looks and hazel eyes drew attention, it was his animated facial expressions that tickled us. That and his unique relationship with Glory endeared us to him. Though a skeptic, one too many coincidences had all but convinced him that God had chosen him to ride Glory.

"Now take this horse and..." said Jake as he rolled off instructions to Darryl.

After a pat on the back, Darryl strode toward Glory.

"Riders up!" called the official.

Before Darryl could mount, Jake headed for Glory's stall, attempting to tighten his loosened tongue-tie. Uncooperative at first, Glory finally accepted the cotton cloth which prevents a horse from getting its tongue over the bit. Otherwise the animal would be very difficult to control. I thought it was weird but surmised Jake knew what he was doing.

My mind flashed back once more to Grandpa John, who was particularly drawn to horses with tongue ties.

Are you watching, Grandpa?

Glory leaped forward as Jake heaved Darryl onto the saddle. Jay, holding Glory tightly, swallowed hard, again digging his heels into the soft dirt, trying to keep Glory from running over a horse that was walking by.

A paddock official opened the gate to the racetrack. Without incident, the field of nine thoroughbreds paraded out in numerical order. When they stepped onto the track, the bugle sounded. Goose bumps rose on my arms.

"Hurry," said Rich, as we scrambled out of the paddock in order to see Glory parade before the crowd.

After securing a good place on the rail, I looked up at Rich, thankful for my husband's 'yes' to the inspiration to buy a racehorse. He was caught up in the thrill of the moment, of witnessing the fulfillment of vision, the fruit of obedience, joy unspeakable!

Mid track, the lead pony rider turned his stunning golden Morgan and headed up the track at a trot. The man looked dashing, his gold jacket bottom flapping in the wind. Nine horses obediently followed.

We glanced at our programs, noting names and trainers. Number two looked very sharp. He turned out to be the favorite. Except for a couple of horses, the competition looked mediocre. Glory was by far the biggest and tallest horse, his powerful body charged to run, his proud Roman head thrust toward the wind. The shedding of his winter coat and meticulous care by his grooms changed a mangy ugly horse into an outstanding thoroughbred. Only protruding backbones marred his magnificence.

Jake's haunting words suddenly ran like tickertape. "I keep feeding him more and more but it doesn't put any meat on him!"

I felt an arm around my waist. "The sweat is pouring off Glory but he still looks good," noted Rich.

Glad for the interruption, I replied, "He's so full of energy!"

Darryl dug his heels into the stirrups and nodded toward us. We gave the vee sign.

"It's your day, Glory," I whispered.

Unbelievably, Glory turned and looked at me. He was my baby. This was his debut, the moment I'd dreamed about since receiving the inspiration to buy a racehorse.

My palms grew sweatier by the minute. Out of nowhere popped Jake's crass words "He's a morning glory!"

I didn't need another negative demon! It was enough worrying about Glory jumping too high out of the starting gate, something Jake and Darryl talked about a lot. Darryl said he spent many a sleepless night trying to find the key to Glory's problem. Even scarier was the possibility of him being dumped!

"Jake seemed pretty excited, don't you think," commented Rich.

"Uh, yes," I replied, once again grateful to be jolted out of abject fear.

Gathering my thoughts, I added, "Jake knows our vision and has been projecting great things to happen, no matter how negative he acts."

"Go For His Glory!" shouted some voices behind us.

I turned to see my two dear friends, Mildred and Helen. Their voices drew the attention of bystanders, who immediately glanced at their programs, presumably looking for Glory's particulars.

"I'll get our tickets," waved Rich who took off for the clubhouse.

"Follow me," I called to my friends.

We made our way up the grandstand and searched for an unobscured view of the finish line. I was getting concerned that Rich hadn't returned.

The horses are nearing the starting gate," called the announcer.

Suddenly, Rich was at my side. I looked into his eyes and he back to mine.

"It's not our show, honey," I said. "It's God's. If Glory does well, that would be wonderful. If not, so be it. That's my philosophy. Of course, like anyone else, I want to see him win."

Rich acceded, his gentle brown eyes telling all, in full agreement to fate.

Simultaneously, we turned to catch the often-hidden action behind the starting gate.

"Use these," said Rich as he handed me his binoculars.

The gate crew was wrapping their arms around Glory's hindquarters, trying to move him closer to the number seven slot. He balked and they lost him, trying again and again. One of the handlers threw up his right hand, grimacing, obviously in pain and shouting an expletive...moving me to stronger prayer and more nail biting.

I shot a glance at Rich. "Did you bet for us?"

He held up the tickets. "Right here!"

Finally, Glory was in the seven chute and the back gate slammed shut. Even then, he reared slightly before quieting. *If only Darryl can hold him...*

As the starting gate clanged open, an audible voice inside me spoke, "This is the birth of a vision."

Rich's hand suddenly clasped mine...a sense of spiritual oneness overwhelming us.

"Did you feel that?" I asked.

"Yes," he said tenderly.

As soon as I repeated the words heard within, the horses sailed out of the starting gate.

"And there're off!" shouted the track announcer.

"Go Glory! You're God's horse! You can do it!" whispered Mildred and Helen.

"For His Glory trails," called the announcer after the first turn.

At the stretch run, I hard squeezed Rich's hand. Glory was beginning to move up and pass other horses. We let go of each other, our arms stretched out.

"Come on Glory, MOVE!" yelled my husband.

I turned to Helen and Mildred but they had disappeared.

A quick look at the tote board showed Glory's odds at twenty to one. We had saved everything we could for this race. It was the most extravagant amount we had ever bet, a hundred dollars across the board.

That meant if Glory placed first, second, or third we would win betting and purse money. If he made fourth or fifth, we would at least make some purse money.

"For His Glory" is in fifth place and making a move," called the track announcer.

Even fifth place would at least pay the jock fee, I thought.

The tension was unbearable. My insides were shaking uncontrollably; a feeling that would be with me every time we raced.

No one would catch the first two horses. That was evident. But suddenly, there was a battle for third, fourth and fifth place. Darryl laid his whip on Glory, asking him, using his hands to encourage him. Glory responded and picked up speed.

"For His Glory is closing and is now in fourth place," called the announcer.

Everyone was yelling for their favorite horses when an unusual phenomenon occurred. As the horses neared the finish line, the roar of the crowd waned rather than increased. Soon, only those calling Glory's name were heard.

At the wire, For His Glory stretched out his head, nipping the fourth-place runner to place third.

You'd think we'd won the Kentucky Derby! Our horse's supporters whooped it up for several minutes after the race was over. There were certainly lots of stares. It was great!!

Rich and I scrambled downstairs to wait for the race to be made official. Along the way, we met Mildred and Helen, their words barely coherent.

"Let's try this one more time," I suggested.

Helen's face glowed. "To get closer to the finish line, we went down this aisle of reserved seats, ending up in the very front row, right over the finish line!"

"Yes," interjected Mildred. "We were screaming, Praise the Lord! You're God's horse! Come on Glory!"

"Anyways," continued Helen, "A little old man with a cigar was standing right below us. He kept turning and giving us dirty looks. After Glory crossed the finish line, the cigar popped out of his mouth and he said aloud, "Well, praise the Lord." We laughed so hard we were crying."

Rich and I marveled about the three events, the third-place finish, the quieting of the crowd to hear Glory's name, and Mildred and Helen's experience with the old man. Added to these was everyone's gratefulness the rain didn't show up. What more could anyone has asked on opening day?

"Here's our money," laughed my husband.

In his hand was $97.50.

Not too bad for a third-place finish, we agreed.

"And we get third place purse money too," I added.

Together, we went to check on Glory.

Jake was waiting for us. "He did great for his first race. I'll see when we can enter him next. Who knows what this horse can do if he'll just settle down and gain some weight?"

"That was an unbelievable finish," I commented.

"Yep. Everything looks fine and you get a paycheck too," he added.

"Sounds good to us. And how much do we tip the help," asked Rich.

While Jake and Rich discussed business, I walked toward Glory. He was on the walker, looking incredibly tired and horribly skinny in his wetsuit!

"You did it, big boy," I told him aloud.

He barely acknowledged me.

"Congratulations!" said Jay and Janice as they came out of the tack room.

"Thanks," I said.

"Yeah," said Rich joining us.

We turned to see Jake staring at Glory.

"Jake is pensive," observed Jan.

"Like he's planning ahead?" suggested my husband.

"Those wheels are turning," I replied.

Life was getting very exciting. Especially jaw-dropping was the next day's newspaper headlines noted by the pic below.

In the beginning...

CHAPTER NINE

CLOSE TO A MIRACLE

As the season raced along, 'For His Glory' had yet to make it to the winner's circle. Thankfully, a few fourth and fifth place finishes were incentive enough to believe for the ultimate. However, any thought of an easy ride to victory lane was about to be shattered.

It started one Saturday morning after Rich and I arrived at the track. The dark, gloomy day turned even gloomier when we found Glory missing from his stall. Instead, a beautiful gray mare was noisily chomping oats. Worst scenarios blazed through my mind.

"What happened?" I questioned aloud.

Rich scanned the shed row. "Your guess is as good as mine."

Routinely, we headed for the gap, past the 'meat cart', where horses are destroyed. Thank goodness it was empty. Now to find Jake…

"Over here!" he called from the far end of his trainer friend's barn.

"Probably pitching in for Stacy," I suggested.

Jake was bent over, doing up a mare's leg. We waited until he stood, an ominous stare piercing us. With clenched jaw and eyebrows raising behind a wave of silver tipped hair, he spoke.

"Your horse injured his back ankle… had to be shipped back to the ranch early this morning. Don't know the extent of the injury, but I've never seen one run after this kind of injury. The vet's probably out there right now."

I froze, wrestling with the possibility our horse might never race again.

Jake shrugged. "Forget the horse! Visions… Huh!"

Jake returned to bandaging the star-browed mare.

Was this a nightmare? Would a pinch wake me up? One thing was sure. Jake's rugged façade could not hide profound disappointment.

Obviously familiar with equine injuries, he spoke from experience. My mind raced, cynicism trying to 'steal' the testimony of several months' work.

Finished with the mare, Jake walked past us toward the men's restroom. Without looking back, he spoke, "Vet's probably out there right now. You might want to check with him later."

"We'll get there soon as we can," promised my husband.

It was late afternoon before we pulled into Jake's driveway. The sky was threatening rain and I was struggling with God, trying desperately to maintain faith in the face of potential disaster. No longer a neophyte, I knew the process of spirituality included obstacles that tested one's faith, exposing the intents of the heart. I finally realized there was only one thing to do.

Tugging at Rich's shoulder, I pleaded, "We have to give Glory back to the Lord?"

Rich's steady blue eyes shifted to the small training track...where Glory learned to be a racehorse.

As I pained for my man, an amazing assuredness filled me with peace. I surrendered to God's will, whatever that entailed. Afterwards, deep within, came the words

"Vision held too tightly allows it to become an idol, usurping the place of the Almighty."

Though sober, the words were balm to my aching heart. I was committed to serving God's purpose at the track, to share His love with all. There was never a guarantee how long this adventure would last or if there would be financial benefits. My only task was to yield to God so He could do His perfect work in and through me.

I looked at Rich, sensing he was also was putting Glory on the altar. No words were needed.

We grabbed two umbrellas as heavy rain began to pelt the windshield. Traversing the outskirts of Jake's largest pasture, we searched for our horse.

"There he is!" pointed Rich.

Looking quite dejected, Glory stood half way out of a small lean-to. I was glad he had protection from the elements since Jake's other pastures had little cover, save for a few trees.

"Glory, come on boy?" I called out.

He barely lifted his eyelids. The disinterest shocked me. I held up an apple treat and still no response.

A large bay suddenly stepped from behind the shed. It brushed Glory's rear, forcing him to move.

I gulped as Glory limped pathetically four or five steps, and then only because he was forced.

In a stupor, we searched for Jake. He was standing on little Joe's porch, his arms animated. We knew how close the two were, sharing the disappointments and joys of thoroughbreds.

"Wonder if Jake received the vet report yet?" commented Rich.

Jake spied us and waved, then walked our way, limping more than usual.

"His poor body...especially those knees," I moaned.

"Years of breaking horses," replied Rich.

We waved at little Joe and steeled ourselves for the news.

"My vet couldn't help your horse. He did suggest, though, that with your permission, we should send for a specialist."

"What do you think our chances are?" I asked.

"Just have to wait and see," he replied. "I've never seen a thoroughbred race after this kind of injury."

Rich thought for a moment and replied, "We'll talk to the group and let you know."

Jake threw up a hand and answered, "Good! It can't hurt anything. The specialist we're thinking about is the best around. If he can't help, no one can."

Armed with a smidgeon of hope and bracing ourselves for the worst, we headed home.

Calls to the group that night were positive. We had nothing to lose but a vet fee.

"We'll go for it," I told Jake the next morning.

"Good...Doc Soster is the best!"

"What do you think our chances are?" I asked.

Jake hesitated. "Just have to wait… never seen a horse race again after this kind of injury…"

I was tired of those words.

The next two days dragged. Finally, the awaited call came.

"Hey, this is Jake. Would you consider an experimental procedure that's never been used on a horse with Glory's injury? Without it, there's no hope."

Once again, the group decided to go for it. The road seemed clear and the expenditure, which had been our chief concern, turned out to be minimal.

Jake was pleased. "Good! Doc Soster will come soon as he can. If the experimental procedure happens to work, he said it would be of interest to other veterinarians. They want to be kept informed about the future of your horse."

Maybe…. just maybe… this was not the end of Glory's career. Hope is wonderful!

It took two more days before Doc Soster made it to Jakes. He injected Glory's ankle and told Jake to let him know how the gelding was getting along.

Within a week Glory was not only walking but tearing around the pasture. Within three weeks, he was in training and shipped back to the track.

"I'm entering him in a race but don't expect anything," phoned Jake one night.

Sober but expectant, the group gathered for prayer before the race, not for a winner, but that Glory's ankle hold up. He ran last, but came back without incident.

"It's really something how Doc's shot worked," exclaimed Jake afterwards at the barn.

"Pretty close to a miracle," winked Rich.

Jake smiled wide, rare for the old codger.

Three precarious weeks saw a doomed horse resurrected and running.

No one, including Jake, could deny an unseen force was intervening in the affairs of men, even caring for a lowly racehorse.

CHAPTER TEN

FINALLY IN THE WINNER'S CIRCLE
BUT SHOULDN'T BE

Jake was having trouble finding a suitable race for Glory. In the meantime, I spent a lot of time with Delores, my dear friend and encourager. She was one of the few who understood my ministry as she had a similar one in the Arabian horse world. We started hearing that churches we never even attended were saying "I'd "gone off the deep end!" That's when we fully realized that implementing vision is an amazing but bizarre world to most people.

"Do your thing at the farm," encouraged Delores one morning after leaving Veronica and Monica to play with her children and ride their pony.

Arriving at the track, I found Jake talking with Glory's farrier. Rather than disrupt, I visited some 'horse friends,' mostly fillies and geldings as stallions intimidated me.

"Renee, I'm free now," called Jake when I returned.

Suddenly, he kicked his foot into the air and cursed!

"I'm going to fire her!!" he yelled.

Usually considerate in my presence, I was at a loss for this sudden outburst. It was particularly disheartening to find that our groom and partner, Jennifer, was again the object of his tirade. I swallowed hard, knowing she would soon be gone.

Jake eventually stopped ranting and pointed to his house. "Let's go inside!" he said.

I followed, surprised at the sudden invitation.

Deenie greeted us with a pot of coffee. "I've felt better than ever since that day," she said, pointing to her back.

"God is good, you know?" I answered; still amazed at her healing.

She shot a glance at Jake then back at me.

He feigned deaf ears and reached for the morning paper.

Deenie set an attractive plate piled high with snicker doodles before us and disappeared into a back bedroom.

"I was an alcoholic till five years ago," offered Jake once again.

He sipped some coffee then eyed me. "Went to AA and have been sober ever since."

"That's wonderful," I answered.

"Got to be the same old stuff so I didn't go back to the meetings. I knew I'd never touch the stuff again."

"Do you know there are good follow-up programs?" I suggested.

"Too tired, too old and too busy, in that order," he replied.

I bit into my snicker doodle.

Jake went on. "We never had kids, you know? These horses are my life… and Deenie? Well, she's a pretty good woman… though she's getting awfully forgetful nowadays."

Jake suddenly rose from his chair and yawned. "I'm going to take a catnap."

I said goodbye and drove back to Delores', pondering Jake's life.

As Labor Day approached, telltale signs of the end of racing season popped up. Trailers pulled out with horses headed for tracks with less competitive fields. Stakes horses went for bigger purse money while marginal winners aimed at stakes races. Notwithstanding travel costs, expenses would be less.

As for our group, we half-heartedly discussed Glory's future. Optimistic Jake often threw in random hints. But we were still in fear mode, wondering if our horse would hold up. On the other hand, the hope of another race that season lingered in our thoughts.

Rich and I arrived at the track one morning, a heavy mist punctuating the crisp autumn air. Bright green leaves had morphed to copper and gold. Once brilliant plants had lost their luster.

Jake seemed happier than usual and greeted us warmly. "I think Glory would do well the other side of the mountains.

He's in good shape and I've had horses that really like the turf there."

We stopped short, realizing Jake's hints regarding Glory's future had to be addressed. A decision had to be made. Thankfully, the winter track he suggested was drivable. Owners want winners but also want to attend their races. Besides, my Uncle Leo lived nearby and would surely come and see us run.

Jake turned pensive, his eyes cast down. He kicked a dirt clod and looked up. "But first, I want to enter him in one more race. It's on Friday's card."

I glanced at my husband, sensing he should make the decision.

Rich stared at the walker, filled with horses dripping from their morning gallop. "Okay, I'm sure the others would be fine with it, too."

Jake pulled a lead chain off a nail and spoke. "Whole stables have moved to other tracks. That makes for smaller fields on the daily racing card, thus more chance of us placing."

"Sounds good," replied Rich.

"We'll see you at the workout Wednesday morning," I added.

Sunshine greeted us as we climbed into the car for Glory's workout. By the time we reached the track, heavy clouds had rolled in. Rich retrieved heavy jackets from the trunk and we started for the gap, a strong nippy wind chilling our faces.

I turned to see our partners pulling into the parking lot. We joined them and headed to the guinea stand, arriving none too early as Jake was ahead of schedule.

Darryl immediately rode by, nodding to us while talking to Glory and rubbing his shoulder. Once on the track, Glory tossed his head, seemingly defying the strong north wind.

"He looks sharp," I commented.

"Sleek and firm," agreed Rich.

The workout went well but a forecast of inclement weather the next few days put us on edge.

"See you Friday," said Jake.

"Absolutely," said Jennifer who had came by to watch the work.

"How are things going?" I asked.

"Jake fired me so I'll have to look for other work, maybe a different field."

"I'm sorry…" I mumbled.

"Me too, but I can't do anything about it."

Tears came as I hugged her.

By late afternoon the rains arrived with a vengeance. They battered the track steadily for two days, deepening the mud. Some horses love an off track; some put up with it, and some just refuse to run. It is not uncommon to see horses break down on bad tracks. I wondered how jockeys had the wherewithal to ride in such horrible conditions. None of us could predict how Glory would take to an off track. Thus far, his races had always been on a fast one.

It was eight o'clock Thursday night, the eve of the race, our phone constantly busy. The group agreed. We would not chance our horse getting hurt or in a mishap. After his injury, it wasn't worth taking the chance. This race was not an option for our 'baby'. We called Jake with the demand to scratch him from the race.

Friday morning, Rich decided to take the day off and go to the track, whether or not we ran. We headed for the barn as there was a break from the rain.

Glory greeted us with an unusually short whinny that I raved about for days! After watching him chomp on his usual carrot treat, we searched for Jake. He was nowhere to be found. The morning help seemed oddly busy so there was none of the usual small talk.

"Let's grab a bite of breakfast," I said.

Rich rubbed his stomach and agreed.

We walked to the backstretch kitchen, ordered coffee and our usual bacon, eggs and hash browns. At the table was a copy of the morning newspaper, opened to the sports section. I flipped the page and my eyes fell on the race card. After noting the horses in the first two races, I dug into my hash browns and proceeded down the list.

"Oh my God! Glory's entered in the third race today!"

Rich's coffee spilled as he reached for the paper that fell from my hands.

"How could he do this?" I ranted. "He didn't pay two cents worth of attention to what we told him to do!"

My husband flushed, looking as furious as I felt. It was too late to go back to the barn and complain to a trainer that was not even around. On second thought, was this the reason everyone at the barn appeared unusually busy?

We looked at each other and spoke in unison, "The Racing Secretary's office!"

It was a short walk to the small building, a hubbub for racing matters. We headed for the front desk, which was lined with owners, trainers and grooms. Trainers were submitting their horses for a race, anxiously waiting for the spinning of ping-pong balls. Anticipation mounted as the Secretary pulled out a ball and announced the horse's name and its post position. I never tired of the experience.

"If you'd like to sit here and wait," I'll get the Secretary when he's done", suggested a clerk.

"Yes, we would," replied my husband.

After several minutes, tall and dignified Josten Howell, the most prominent figure at the racetrack, with exception of its owner, walked in. Howell wrote articles for the town paper and, of course, the daily racing form. A fixture at the track, Grandpa John admired the Howell family as they were pioneers in the town.

"Hi, I'm Josten Howell," he said with a handshake.

"Nice to meet you," we said.

Rich presented our case and we awaited his response.

Howell turned serious. "Yes, it is indeed your right not to race your horse and I will talk to him about it."

Feeling quite smug, we walked to our car and drove home. Yes, we could not stop Jake from racing Glory, but the result was in his hands. If the horse got hurt...well...he would pay!

I quickly called the group. Stress mounted as they adjusted work schedules to attend the race. By early afternoon the rain had stopped and a warm sun appeared. We dressed and waited for the afternoon card.

A later call found the track changed from sloppy to muddy. That was a relief, though confronting Jake was still foremost in our minds.

By the time we arrived at the track, its condition changed from mud to slow. That was good, though but possibly deceptive, because it might be slippery beneath the dry surface. Our partners were anxious too. Glory was their first interest in a thoroughbred and they loved him and didn't want him hurt again. Jennifer was especially nervous about the turnaround.

Another concern was Glory's drawing post position number two. Because the grade of the track slants slightly toward the rail, a rail position is a negative since it dries slower. Horses tend to bog down and come up short. At least Glory was not in the first hole. Of that, we were thankful.

We met Jake coming through the gap. Making our way across the infield, we addressed our concerns. Glory was jumping around so much, our words floated into oblivion.

In the paddock, we marveled that he saddled well, not his usual nervous self. Jake didn't bother to come over, obviously ignoring our concerns.

As the bugle sounded, the horses and their jockeys paraded onto the track.

We hustled up the stairs of the clubhouse and looked for a good vantage point to catch the post parade action. As usual, my heart staged its now familiar palpitations. I was learning to accept exhilaration at the beginning of a race and severe exhaustion at the end. I called the latter my 'horseman's hangover.'

This time, however, below my nerves was excitement beyond belief, as if I was riding in the race.

"The horses are entering the starting gate," called the track announcer.

Glory loaded easily, a relief for all of us.

My body began to shake uncontrollably.

"And they're off!!.... For His Glory is taking the lead."

"The track's not bothering him at all," I said to my husband. "In fact, it looks like he's enjoying it!"

Rich tried to hand me his binoculars but I kept mumbling the words could he possibly win?

"… At the quarter mile pole, 'For His Glory' is still leading by two lengths," called the announcer.

We both yelled as Glory crossed the finish line.

"It's all For His Glory!" shouted the announcer.

My shaking turned to exaltation. Now it was a matter of waiting for the official results. Rich and I nearly flew downstairs, meeting our partners at the bottom. There were plenty of hugs and tears were flowing.

We waited anxiously.

"The results of the third race are now official," declared the announcer.

Elated beyond belief, our group walked into the coveted winner's circle.

Jake came in for the picture and we hugged him. He grinned.

"Sorry about entering without your permission, but I had a feeling about the horse for this race."

At that moment, I caught sight of an overhead message coming down from the big brass. A phone rang. It was for Jake.

When we realized what was happening, we all apologized profusely.

The secretary had severely reprimanded Jake for going against our wishes. For once, we were grateful for his toughness and sticking with his gut instinct, no matter what!

In retrospect, we had yielded to fear. It gripped us to the degree that we took matters into our own hands, a common side effect of 'green owners". Not that caution is unwarranted, but a master is keenly aware when a horse is ready and the timing is right. God had overruled our immature prayers and fears in order to put His horse in the winner's circle. What a great God we have!

Unfortunately, that was not the end of my humiliation. While Rich went to collect the proceeds of our small bet, I headed for Jake's box seats. Shockingly, Maggie greeted me with a severe tongue-lashing. Her guests watched as I died of embarrassment. She had taken the attack on her husband personally and with words not fit for a lady, she rebuked me. I knew I deserved it because faith trusts the Divine hand to work all things for good. Though Jake never said anything about the incident, Maggie was not so quick to forgive and forget...With red face and a pound of humility, I walked with our group to the testing barn where winning horses are checked for illegal drugs. Glory came out fine.

After Jake checked his overall condition and things looked okay, we celebrated at a nearby racehorse friendly restaurant.

CHAPTER ELEVEN

THE TWO-YEAR-OLD FUTURITY

Things seemed fine after Glory's win until a few days later. His left ankle, not the one injured in the first incident, began to swell. Over time it improved enough for Jake to suggest the unbelievable, enter him into biggest race of the year, the Two-Year-Old Futurity!

The option to run was available to us when we purchased Glory. The initial down payment toward the $500 fee was minimal so the necessary paperwork was completed and he was pre-qualified. When he got hurt, we assumed he would never be in contention for the 'big one'. Now, with only a maiden win, he was eligible and Jake wanted us to enter. Whether we placed or not, being able to compete with the finest two-year-olds of the year was a great privilege. Though Jake was overly impressed with Glory's win, in our hearts we knew he did not have a chance.

Oh well, we all agreed; let's go for it anyways!

We paid up, were accepted, and drew the number nine post position.

Excitement mounted as the day grew closer. By this time, there were only two horses left in Jake's barn. The others were hurt, sore, broke down or had died. We realized how fortunate we were in that Glory had gotten this far.

Television cameras zoomed in as we entered the paddock. Familiar faces of the rich and famous surrounded us, a football player, boxer, and TV personality. We felt little but great. Our 'winner' was going against the 'big guys and gals', an emotion impossible to describe.

Glory's body, though still bony, fit in with the elite crop of two-year-olds. Size does not guarantee a good runner but Glory's outstanding body did attract attention. His final odds were seventeen to one, respectable for an unknown with only a maiden win.

The horses loaded well and for the first time I was quiet inside. I knew the odds, no longer a neophyte in racing.

"And they're off!" shouted the announcer.

Glory was last out of the starting gate but moved up slowly through the first turn. Toward the end of the home stretch, he passed three horses in the field of twelve. Our 'baby' did the best he could, tiring at the end and placing ninth.

"Not so bad," said Jake with a nod, "especially since his leg swelled some this morning."

We were shocked at the admission. Should he have run Glory when he was not up to par? How would he have done if totally fit?

Jake read our thoughts. "It wasn't that bad or I wouldn't have run him. Besides, he'll be enjoying the pasture by tomorrow and have plenty of time to mend."

We accepted Jake's assessment and went out for dinner; still amazed he raced in the biggest two-year-old event of the year. And we beat three horses!!

CHAPTER TWELVE

PATIENCE AND JUDGMENT

During a panel talk show, the great philosopher Eric Hoffer once said, "Life is as a play with different acts and changing characters." Young intellectuals on that panel were vehement, unable to accept his evaluation of the scenario of life.

In our youth, we tend to think ourselves self-sufficient, in need of no one. The vibrancy we feel makes it easy to fall into that trap. We think we are the director. Because they are youth, the mature dismiss this foolishness. That's because they know it is foolishness. A resurrected "I can do anything' spirit," tempts us to do what we know we should not do, often ending with disastrous results. I was about to encounter a couple of experiences that would ultimately alter my course at the track.

A light drizzle fell as I arrived at the ranch one morning. Usually, Jake came straight out to meet me, but this day he did not. About to leave, the front door opened and he hobbled toward me.

"What happened?" I asked.

He grimaced, pointing toward the new horse in the barn. "Oh, I got dumped when my rider refused to ride that sucker. This body ain't as young as it used to be. Oh well…."

My first thought was thankfulness he was not badly hurt. Next was the realization that horses can outwit even the best trainer. Riders, especially those who break horses, face many obstacles. It is dangerous work. During his youth, Jake was an exceptionally skilled breaker of horses. In his later years, the job took a toll on his body and he finally succumbed to letting younger men do the job. However, the previous day's incident hit a vulnerable spot in Jake. His youthful ego rose, refusing to accept defeat. Jake the expert had to 'fix the horse!' Unfortunately, it fixed him, right back into reality!

"Have to get some bandages for my filly. I'll be right back," he said as he painfully limped off.

"Okay," I replied, after sensing he wanted me to stay.

My instant reaction was praying for his broken body. On the other hand, doubts as to the condition of his mind pressed heavily on me.

"Hi Renee," called one of the farmhands.

"Hey Juno, how are you doing?"

Juno lifted his burly arms, displayed his biceps, and then hung his arms like a limp rag. "It's been a long morning and I'm about done for."

I turned for a moment to see Jake disappear into a tack room. Juno followed my glance and spoke animatedly.

"You ought to have seen the boss yesterday. He was like a crazy man when Arty refused to ride that mean stud. Said he'd get on the horse and discipline it himself! That (expletive) horse threw him and got him in the side. Had to go to a chiropractor and then get some pain pills. Best thing he done was calling the stud's owner and telling them to pick up their blankety horse. Shouldn't have ridden him…."

I turned back and saw Jake walking out of the tack room, his arms full of bandages. Juno quickly walked away.

"Want to see how to wrap legs?" said Jake.

Yeah, that would be great," I replied, still mulling over Juno's comments.

Jake opened the stall door and went in. It was his favorite horse, a nine-year-old mare he like to talk about. "Never had trouble with this one, the gentlest horse I've ever had. She's run good for me, even a couple of stakes races."

"Wow," I replied. It was the first time Jake had ever allowed me in a stall. He said it was too dangerous and was afraid I would get hurt. The excuse was always the issue of insurance. His restriction the first year was palatable but by the second year, I became somewhat resentful. After all, I had previously owned horses, was no stranger to their habits, and felt his distrust unwarranted. Ultimately, though, God was holding things back. He knew how much I loved horses. He also knew I needed growth in virtue, which usually does not come easily.

The coveted time I had longed for finally arrived, the privilege of seeing a master at work. Because it was winter, crippled horses like this mare had to have constant attention. Otherwise, they would not be ready for racing in the spring.

"First, you rub their neck and tell them what you want to do," he said matter of fact.

As he laid down the bandages with other supplies needed for the job, a great sense of awe overwhelmed me, like the door to Jake's heart was about to open.

He knelt down in the straw. I sat down close to him, glad that grubby jeans and an old jacket were my choice of apparel that morning.

"Next, you have to rub this leg paint on them." He uncapped a dark bottle and tenderly applied the solution. The action surprised me. His usual gruffness belied a tender spirit when it came to actually working with the animals. I had only seen him oversee others while they worked with the horses. Now I understood why everyone called him a beginner's teacher. He enabled greenhorns to learn the trade.

Next, he wrapped plastic wrap around the horse's shins and ankles. After that came thick cotton cloth sheeting. Finally, he applied covering bandages that were wrapped snugly and secured. The whole process took an hour since all four legs were involved. All the while Jake, the teacher, talked and explained what he was doing and why.

I suddenly felt claustrophobic in the twelve by twelve stall, appreciating what a sequestered horse must feel like. The overhead lighting was dim, barely enough to see. In these stalls, most even smaller ones, a racehorse lives some twenty-three hours a day during racing season. It is hardly an easy life, but the calling of this equine athlete.

My senses suddenly heightened, aware that one wrong move can injure or kill a person or cause a hundred thousand dollar horse to be worth zilch. The responsibility is immense and requires tough people capable of a lot of stress. I thought of many like Jake who could retire if they wanted. They are tempted. They told me they were. Nevertheless, when spring came and beautiful flowers peeked out of the earth, they succumbed to the lure and incredible joy of working with these animals. That is what pushed them on, just one more year. Racing is a rare profession in that people can work from early youth to death. Very few who have been in the sport most of their lives quit until they absolutely have to.

Contrary to most professions, there is great respect for old-timers in racing. The richness of their experience is coveted. Serious horse people yearn to glean from those who have paved the way before them.

The job finished, Jake slowly picked himself up off the straw and opened the stall door. I followed, still mesmerized by the experience.

"God is good," I commented.

Jake half grinned. "Without the Almighty I could not have stopped drinking."

"There's so much more to knowing God," I encouraged.

Jake listened then turned toward his house. I left the farm; confident this old man would open his heart and desire a closer relationship with God. Unbeknownst to me, he chose to run the other way.

After that incident, physical problems began to plague me. I was twenty-five years old and had never had allergy problems. Suddenly, severe allergy symptoms erupted. Working in the yard was misery. Episodes happened with no warning. Getting near straw or hay was hell for me.

Meanwhile, Jake became increasingly negative, then downright mean, especially to me. Usually tolerant, I was disgusted with myself, probably because I no longer seemed to have a positive influence in his life. I realized it was not my job to change Jake. It was God's. Still, I could not seem to shake myself from the sense of responsibility. I saw only defeat!

One particular day, the unwelcome allergy symptoms hit me as I drove to the farm. A heavy rash appeared on my upper extremities. My eyes swelled incredibly. I left the farm, daring not to go inside. I really believe that angels helped me drive home.

I writhed in agony for an hour; face down on my bed before getting any relief. God was trying to tell me something about Jake but I was afraid to hear. I finally surrendered. My first trainer, the one who helped me get this far, the one whom I had shared so much, was now my foe. Feeling the sting of this realization, I unleashed the power of God and cried out, "You deal with him! I don't deserve this kind of treatment!"

It took a week to get courage to go back to the farm. Deenie met me outside, which was highly unusual.

"Jake had some kind of a blackout," she said seriously. "He was coming home one night last weekend and crashed his truck into an abutment. They've done all kinds of tests and can find nothing wrong with him."

I stood there stunned, almost shaking from the knowledge that God's power had allowed this. Never had I experienced that kind of answer to prayer. Yet, never had I pronounced that kind of judgment on anyone! I honestly did not think anything earth shattering would happen, but it did.

Though God heard the cry of my heart and meted out his retribution, I did not gloat. Rather, this experience caused me to think twice about ever again asking God to get on someone's back. We do not know the repercussions.

I did not see Jake for several days. He came out of the experience shaken but otherwise unhurt. His attitude changed a bit, as if he knew this was a warning. But his skewed personality and crudeness had taken their toll on me. I thought he was a soul bent for hell. God had different plans for him, however, but that revelation would come to me much later.

CHAPTER THIRTEEN

MOVING ON - ANOTHER STABLE NAME

After the two-year-old championship, Jake called for a horse van and shipped Glory to the farm. Our tired boy deserved a much-needed rest. I found it difficult to say goodbye to the familiar sights and sounds that had now dimmed to an eerie death beat. Missing would be the adrenalin rushes as pounding hooves raced past the finish line. Even the incredible joy of doing God's work was likely to continue at a much slower and quieter pace.

I arrived behind Jake's van and mused as Glory sniffed through his new stall.

"See ya," waved Joe, as he led one of his horses out to pasture.

Left to my thoughts, I nuzzled Glory for a long time, feeling a consuming sadness. Not surprisingly, I was already feeling the void of new friends and acquaintances met over the racing season. It was unlikely I would see them again until spring. My inner balloon was shrinking, losing its last bit of air. Finally, I accepted the curtain dropping and began to anticipate what God might have in store for the next scene.

Daily trips to Jake's became a ritual. The usual boring ten-mile drive was now breathtaking, shining as a freshly painted autumn landscape. The scene was short-lived however. Leaves began to shed and the horses' once sleek bodies turned dull and hairy. Mother Nature had taken over, preparing the animals for the cold winter.

This daily grind took a toll on my family. Most of the day was darkness and I rarely got home before noon. Yet, my enthusiasm and inexhaustible drive toward an unknown destiny prevailed. Eventually, my husband and children stopped feeling left out. They even encouraged me to keep following the train of my inner vision. Thankfully, the hustle and bustle of Christmas holiday preparations kept everyone busy.

For several weeks, a nagging question in my mind kept popping up. How would Glory further glorify God? Yes, he could blossom as a three year old, run in the Kentucky Derby, and become famous. My best friend even wrote a song about that. I knew God rarely does it that way. He had called me at this track and for these people. His original message had not changed -- that the Creator of the Universe wanted horse people to know He loved them."

Some had accepted the message and were already making positive changes in their lives. They realized one of the most precious things a person has is the ability to make God happy. Yet, there were many more who needed this message.

I turned to deep prayer, waiting for a word from the only one that can touch human hearts. The answer to such prayer often clarifies one's calling and the gifts that accompany it. When I received the Divine commission to "Go out and buy a thoroughbred, name him For His Glory, and run in My name," I received the charismatic gift of faith, a strength and power to believe, no matter what. Liken it to a mega dose of vitamins, except the energy is sustained until the vision is completed. It is not just 'hoping' something will manifest, but 'knowing' it will, in His time and His way. It is a wonderful empowerment from on high!

After my meditative experience, peace filled my soul. I received what was needed to continue the journey. After all, there are many temptations and pitfalls in this very worldly industry. The good news is that when God ordains a vision, He is in charge! He wants to 'lead' the way. Moreover, He was about to manifest His lead position once again!

December twentieth was a bleak day. Like most mothers, I was up to my elbows in a sink of dirty dishes. My countenance lifted as the bright sun suddenly peeked out and lit my dark kitchen. It was a welcome relief from the heavy rain that had pelted our home most of the morning.

Veronica, my precious thirteen year old, came rushing into the kitchen. "Mom! Mom! Come look at the rainbow."

We charged into the living room. The rainbow's brilliance was dazzling, especially since the perfect arc was directly in front of our large picture window.

A shiver ran through me. Could it be? Was the rainbow a symbol destined to be on the back of Glory's future silks? A few days previous, I had mused over the thought, wondering if it was God's mind or just my own. What a perfect image, one that never ceases to amaze humankind. The rainbow is a dramatic sign of God's love. It memorializes His covenant with man, that He would never again flood the earth.

"Wow, it's sooo beautiful!" oohed ten-year-old Monica, who had just entered the room. "Mom, I'm going outside to see the ends of the rainbow." Excitedly, she zipped out the door.

I chuckled to myself. We lived on the corner of a cul-de-sac with great firs at either end of the street. Surely, that would preclude anyone from seeing the ends of the rainbow. Once again, I attacked the dirty dishes. Veronica stayed at the front window, spellbound by the display of colors.

A few minutes later, the front door slammed. "Mom!" yelled Monica breathlessly. "There are doves flying around the end of the rainbow!!"

I stared hard at my lovely blonde blue-eyed daughter. "Oh…"

"Yeah, Mom, I saw them, beautiful white doves flying around the ends of the rainbow."

"Let's go see, honey," I said disbelievingly.

We hurried out the door with Veronica on our shirttails. Neither Veronica nor I saw anything. In fact, the once brilliant colors had faded to dim. Nevertheless, that was not important. I had received another inspiration. The rainbow would not be the only image on For His Glory's silks. The green satin fabric would have a rainbow at the top and a white dove below, a symbol of the Old and New Testaments, the old and new covenants. What a revelation for His glory!

The next few days seemed hazy, as if I was in the mind of God, receiving insights about the old and new covenants. Strangely, the contrast of old and new expanded to women in the racing industry. Until recent years, with exception of some wives, racing was a man's world. Now, women were trainers, grooms, exercise riders and even jockeys. Had the intrusion of women in the field made a intrinsic difference?

Curiosity and the need for confirmation sent me out into the field. I sought out old timers, asking them if things were different since women had become more active in racing. Their answer confirmed what I was thinking. Yes, it did produce a softening effect in the industry. Coarse language and all around male harshness were diminished. However, those women pioneers were not softies. On the contrary, they had to be extraordinarily tough to surmount walls of discrimination and jealousy. They were subject to many tribulations and trials, all inherent to progress. Some walked, talked and cussed right along with the men, not always a Christian concept of a woman. Others were tough skinned yet gentle mannered, willing and eager to learn from the bottom up.

A close friend of mine worked with several trainers before she got a job with one considered most prestigious in the field. He eventually became her mentor.

When she went on to become a successful trainer, he continued to share his knowledge of secrets learned over a lifetime. I'm sure it was her gentle spirit and humility which ultimately gained his respect and trust. He wanted to leave behind a worthy legacy and chose a woman.

Another facet of my meditation was the absence of a spiritual gathering place for horse people. After all, I had grown to realize the world of the backstretch was its own little city. This city had real people with real problems and little professional help, if any. Where was the church in this forgotten city?

I had been into horse racing over a year when I heard about a group of Christians who had a burden for their fellow workers. What a relief to hear I was not alone! Others in the field had seen an enormous gap and aggressively moved toward filling it. In fact, this group of racetrack workers was actively trying to get funding for a chaplain! More amazing was that they were trying to get the major funding from the racetrack establishment! I was amazed at their grassroots work and soon joined them for weekly meetings.

The group agreed that churches should not disregard the thoroughbred racing industry just because gambling is involved. Most were involved with a church that not only prayed for race trackers but also backed their members' missionary efforts. They realized that launching a faith body that would enable horse people to have Sunday church right at the track was an exciting pioneer mission. Marriages could take place and study groups formed. Sermons could be geared to horsemen. Race trackers need God like anyone else. They need to know that Jesus died for them, too. All should have the choice to accept or reject the Lord of the Universe, but how can they know Him unless someone tells them? I was grateful to be a small part of this great move of God.

Before meeting this group of genuinely caring race trackers, I had an experience that didn't make a lot of sense at the time. The experience happened one morning during racing season. Usually, I had parked on the east side of the track, but for some reason, that morning I parked on the north side. I was walking toward my car, about a hundred feet from the tall, wide gate that was the main entry to the backstretch. Suddenly I saw an image, a day vision. Behind the closed gate was a huge white horse and rider. The white horse's breast was level with the gate, about eight feet high. I presumed Jesus to be riding the white horse. Coiled across the whole length of the top of the gate was a huge serpent. The white horse then lifted one foot as if to strike the serpent. Suddenly, the scene was over. I shuddered at the experience, sharing it only with a couple of people.

A short time later, I saw a continuation of the white horse scene. This time, the horse struck the serpent, the gate opened, and horse and rider walked in.

I knew Jesus was going to do something, but I didn't know what. Now the meaning was clear. There was going to be church at the racetrack and nothing and no one could stop it.

After meeting with my newfound group, I realized this is what the vision meant, that a church would indeed come forth. This day vision was also a sober reminder to me that a call to racetrack work or ministry must be carefully discerned. Temptations abound, especially to compromise one's beliefs. The burden of financial lack or fear of lack can tempt one to use unethical practices with horses or in dealings with owners. Alcoholism, drug addiction and gambling certainly are issues. Yet, I found many wonderful caring people who worked hard and treated their horses and owners justly. I must admit though, that some had to leave the industry for their own welfare or that God had other plans for their lives. It is critical that we follow the leading of the Holy Spirit or we may be on our own!

The year ended peacefully and a light January snow dotted the landscape. One late afternoon, Rich and I headed to Jake's for a meeting with our other owners. Up to then, the racing form and track program listed the group's personal names as Glory's owners. Any effort on my part to suggest otherwise wound up at a dead-end. I was clear as to the direction we were supposed to go and wondered if the time was finally right.

During the quiet drive, neither of us spoke. My mind drifted to a time before even signing Glory's purchase papers, to the days soon after the original inspiration to buy Glory. I needed to know the basis for my vision at the track. Revelation 6.2 came to me. It would be my anchor in regards to the racetrack vision. It reads:

"To my surprise I saw a white horse, its rider had a bow, and he was given a crown.

He rode forth victorious, to conquer yet again." Rev 6:2 NAB

I interpreted this to mean that Glory was going to win some races and that God was 'riding' this process. His purpose and plan would be accomplished and acknowledged. Other than this assessment, I was in the dark as to the scripture's full meaning.

Then came my dilemma, the teaching in religious circles that cast the white horseman's rider as the evil one. This was too big for me. I had accepted the call to the racetrack and never looked back but I knew I was now on dangerous ground. I checked back with God and He said the same thing. HE was coming on the white horse! Okay God, I believe you but…. for my own peace and sanity I need confirmation of what I heard.

My Restoration Pastor and bible teacher, whom I respected enough to accept his interpretation for this scriptural passage, was contacted. A luncheon date was planned and we soon looked eye to eye.

Pastor Gregorn was a strong husky man of German origin. Even though I received inspiration and power from his teaching ministry, he did not support my call to race track ministry. In fact, he said I'd go to hell if this mission wasn't of God! Of course, he said it gently, and loved me despite my 'off track' mission. Who else would God speak through than one adamantly opposed to my mission? Yet, I knew and was ready to accept his interpretation. I have to admit that I was expecting the same answer as the commentaries and most churches taught.

"Pastor, who is the white horseman in Revelation 6.2?"

My dear friend looked at me for a moment, and then answered. "I know most believe him to be the evil one. But, according to Dake's Bible, it is Christ! I concur with that."

I was shocked! Pastor Gregorn did not know why I had asked the question. He had no idea I was considering it for our stable name.
Armed with this Pastor's shocking answer, I was ready to face the world…and Rich. He had no trouble accepting our discernment.

"We're here, honey," chimed my husband as we drove up Jake's driveway. I gathered my wits and greeted the rest of our group who had already arrived.

"We think it's time to design these silks you're talking about," said one of our partners.

"I believe there should be a rainbow and dove on them," I replied, "And can we also talk about another stable name?"

"Shoot," replied the partner.

"Revelation Six-Two is the one I would like. Do you all concur?"

The room was quiet. Jake and our other partners looked at each other.

"I need for you to know we've been offered another piece of Glory," said one of the partners.

My husband and I looked at each other, a little stunned.

"Okay," said my husband. "Now there are only two of us, right?"

Jake's eyes never left the table. He obviously wanted out of ownership of Glory. With everyone agreed on the silks and stable name, we shook hands and left.

The ride home was sobering, yet exciting. I had dreamed of the day Glory would be all ours. Now the opportunity was a little closer. We would just have to wait.

The next few days were a blur. Choosing material, a dressmaker and designer for the emblems were more of a project than I realized. Soon, things came together and I was telling everybody about what was transpiring. Unfortunately, that is not always wise.

It happened one morning as I dashed through a department store looking for sales. I met the pianist from Pastor Gregorn's church. Rather than her usual soft response after my greeting, she tore into me!

"How can you shame God by identifying Him with a horse like "For His Glory" and putting a blanket on him with a rainbow and dove!!"

"Ah…" I stammered.

"How could you do that?" she repeated vehemently.

"That's was I was called to do, to bring the gospel to them," I replied gently."

The woman stomped off, leaving me with the distinct feeling that my friend was right. She had said many churches had spiritually cast me into the ocean with the devil! That mantle of faith I mentioned earlier shielded me from this woman's accusations. Normally, I would have crumbled in such an encounter. Thank God for His manifold graces and the power to move on.

Bless those who persecute you; bless and do not curse.   Rom 12:14

CHAPTER FOURTEEN

THE HARD ROAD - VISION AT THE BARN GATE

Glory was racing across the fields, his legs solid after bouts of swelling. That sparked a light in Jake. It was his signal that Glory was sharp, suggesting he did not need the extended winter season to recoup. "Horses talk to you," he often said. Glory was talking!

Hence, a call from Jake one evening. "I'd like you to come out tomorrow. Have something to propose to you."

It was a bitterly cold Saturday morning. I dressed warmly, complete with long underwear, a hat and mittens. Even my husband, who rarely ever wore a hat, did so and brought his leather gloves. We ran the car's engine for several minutes then drove out to the ranch.

Jake greeted us with a shudder. "Brrrr, colder than Alaska, and I'm wearing two woolen shirts under this jacket!"

We walked toward Glory's stall, shivering as a strong gust of north wind whipped by. Little breath clouds dotted the air as we spoke.

"Rather than waiting for racing season, I think you should run Glory at Meadow Downs. The big guy will like the surface there and have a better chance of winning. The day money is less, too.

We were surprised, almost at a loss for words. Jake waited a moment then added, "I'll be staying here at the ranch, but I'll give you a trainer referral."

The challenge was intriguing. Meadow Downs was across the state, easily drivable, save for snow. Glory would run mid January rather than wait for May. Since it was financially feasible, our partners had no problem with Jake's suggestion. With that in mind, we happily agreed.

Ironically, Jake's trainer referral turned out to be Dusty Liken, his former groom's boss, the man I wished Jake would be like. This made easier an otherwise awkward transition. God answered our prayers. Once the break came, we never returned to Jake.

"I think I can do well for you," avowed Dusty at our first meeting. Heavyset and in his seventies, he walked with a strong limp.

Dusty lived alone in a small trailer behind the track, a definite advantage for someone handicapped.

He was well liked, often referred to as one of the old-timers of the industry. His gentleness and knowledge of horses is what impressed us. Peace had finally descended upon us, a rare commodity the last several months.

A few days later, Jake telephoned. "Glory shipped over fine. In fact, he's eating up the track like he never did here!"

A tinge of guilt crept over me. We all felt bad about leaving Jake. On the other hand, we could not deny the overwhelming peace that came after meeting with Dusty.

He wasted no time and soon called with the news. "I've entered Glory in a race. Can you make it here this weekend?"

This weekend' was only three days away! With a little juggling, we made the trip. Thankfully, the forecast of snow in the mountains did not materialize. Our initial enthusiasm dimmed, however, when Glory ran last.

A week later, the phone rang again. I've entered Glory in a lower class race."

"You know, Dusty, I don't think any of us can make it. Will you call and tell us what happens?"

"Absolutely," he replied.

Dusty did call, only to give us the news that Glory finished next to last. Our dreams had turned from bad to worse. Now, Dusty suggested the inevitable--dropping Glory to the lowest possible claiming race. With such a poor showing thus far, surely no one would claim him, our biggest fear. Besides, last and next to last finishes were not worth the two hundred mile drive. We had been humbled to the max!

"He got in the race," phoned Dusty.

We made the best of the situation and drove east for the 'dirt cheap' race. It was a clear crisp day and even a few familiar faces showed up. After studying the racing form, Glory definitely outclassed the other entries. Bettors saw his ratings, too. Suddenly, he was the favorite on the tote board. That felt strange. This was the first time we had ever been in the limelight before a race.

An extra special bonus of the trip was our jockey. He was a delightful young man we had become acquainted with at Century Downs. An apprentice, George was looking for his first win. Glory was primed for the race and his number one post position was definitely to his advantage.

As the horses loaded in the starting gate, my stomach filled with butterflies. Glory flew out of the gate and immediately took the lead. I bit my lip. I knew he was going to win.

"It's all For His Glory!" shouted the announcer. The excitement we felt was almost as great as the first race he had won. It had been a long haul. The inferior purse did not matter. A win was a win!

"Congratulations, George!" shouted our group. A champagne bottle popped and the announcer praised the grinning jockey for breaking his maiden (celebrated after a jockey wins his first race). The crowd responded with cheers and some clapping. What a privilege for us and For His Glory!

The trip back home was joyous. There was a little money in our pockets and great anticipation for what lay ahead.

The next week Dusty called again. "I entered Glory in the next class. Unfortunately, he did not get in. I had to put him in a higher claimer. We can't wait another week. He's too fit not to run."

Shock hit us all. The class was even higher than the duds where Glory had come last and next to last. His chances were zilch. I looked up to God and surrendered my will, "He is your horse. I have to realize you may just want me to meet or minister to someone." Yes, we would make the trip anyways.

The weather the week of the race was blustery, a steady stream of rain falling. We packed and took off for the Friday afternoon card. It would be a family oriented weekend since we were invited to stay overnight with my uncle Leo and aunt Margaret. Usually, we went straight home after the races or stayed at a hotel near the track.

The scenery in our state varies. On the west side, there are beautiful mountains, streams and fertile valleys. On the east side are barren brown hills. Yet, even those barren hills show signs of God's handiwork. I especially enjoyed the change of pace from big town to small town. Missing are traffic jams, factories, and jet noise!

We parked our car, passed the guard gate, and walked toward Dusty's barn.

It was the furthest back of the five hundred stalls that dotted the park. With exception of horses preparing for the afternoon race card, the backstretch was deserted. That always felt strange to me since mornings burst with so much activity.

"Well, he's feeling real good," said Dusty chewing on his unlit pipe.

"Sure is," assured the groom.

Glory looked great, though his bones still protruded heavily through his sleek body. I missed the pompoms. Dusty was not much for decorating his horses. More than anything else, we were anxious to see the new silks on our jockey, finished a short time before the race. I knew the extraordinary design would provide new opportunities for me to share God's love with race trackers.

The backstretch PA system interrupted. "Horsemen, please bring your horses up for the third race."

We walked alongside Glory to the gap. After that, we separated. Horses and their handlers went to the right. The rest of us walked to the left, a narrow path across the infield. This measure was for our protection. Within a couple of minutes, a very scary scene would give us even more respect for this rule.

We were half way across the infield when the horse ahead of Glory suddenly panicked, kicking one of the handlers in the head. The boy was dazed and taken with assistance back to the first aid station. As mentioned before, working around these high-spirited animals is dangerous. Racehorses are especially edgy before a race. Many are given extra vitamins for maximum performance. Later, we heard the handler suffered a bad concussion.

After the unnerving experience in the infield, we entered the paddock. Soon, it was abuzz with owners and trainers eyeing the competition. The class in the race intimidated us. A couple of the horses had even run in allowance races.

The door to the jockeys' room opened. Our new rider's name was Danielle, a petite brown haired girl in her early twenties. She greeted us and spun around to show off the silks.

"They do look great, don't they." she said with a big smile.

The green satin shone like an emerald. We marveled at the beautifully embroidered rainbow and white dove. They looked magnificent! Of course, we were just a tad prejudiced....

Dusty agreed to give Danielle a chance to ride since we had little hope to place. I was glad Dusty was open to women riders. Though Jake never said he had a problem with them, as far as I know, he never used one.

"Riders up," called the announcer.

I walked out of the paddock straight to our favorite viewing site. My husband went to bet our now common six-dollar across the board bet.

"And they're out of the gate," called the track announcer.

Glory broke well from his ninth post position. He passed a couple of horses on the backside. On the final turn, he started to move up.

"For His Glory is making a move. He's now in fourth place," chimed the announcer.

I got excited. "Come on Glory, get up there in front!"

"Go Glory!!" shouted my husband.

The exhilaration was unbelievable. Glory was moving, and fast! Danielle used her whip strategically, demanding every ounce of strength from her mount.

I looked at the tote board. Glory was going at seventeen to one.

"For His Glory is making a move to the front. He is passing them all. It is all "For His Glory"!

We jumped up and down, trying to contain ourselves. I thanked God. We had been greatly humbled only to be blessed beyond belief. The crowd was stunned as their favorite ceded to an obscure horse named 'For His Glory'!

The family dinner was wonderful, often punctuated by comments from my Uncle Leo about the race. Though he was not a racing fan, he decided to come and support us anyways. Aunt Margaret shared the whereabouts of her seven children, most of them in the medical field.

With the winter racing season almost over, we considered bringing Glory home earlier than planned. He had done well and we wanted to save him for later. Extremely cold weather clinched our decision as they called off the races.

With the winter racing season almost over, we considered bringing Glory home earlier than planned. He had done well and we wanted to save him for later. Extremely cold weather clinched our decision as they called off the races.

With a successful season behind us, we looked for a place to winter our winner. After arranging his care at a friend's farm, we settled down, assuming this transition would be easy until...

CHAPTER FIFTEEN

THE DREAM

Ray, a neighbor friend sold his home and bought acreage so he could board thoroughbreds. Our group decided it would be a great place to board Glory after his two-year-old racing year. That way, I could handle him to my heart's content.

When a thoroughbred comes off the racetrack, they are kept in a stall for three days in order to wind down. By the third day of being cooped up they are obviously crazy to get out. I would be the one to go in and unloose Glory's halter before opening the stall door. It would be scary because they are big animals and can run over you. When the door opens, they shoot out.

That night I had a violent dream. Not being much of a dreamer, it scared the living daylights out of me. I saw Glory let out into the small arena outside his stall, crash through the fence and die!

Panicked when I awoke, I quickly dialed Ray.

"No problem, Renee," I'll open the gate to the big pasture.

I dressed and headed out to the ranch. The gate to the aforementioned pasture was open. Glory would hopefully sail out of his stall and see that opening.

I prayed I would be able to free him as he was so jumpy, pumped to get out of his stall.

"I know Glory, how much you need to get out," I said, as I eased my way into the stall and removed his halter. My body trembled as my shaking hands slowly opened the door. I jumped aside in time to feel the weight of his body rush past me. Glad to survive what only a seasoned horseman should be doing, I held my breath.

Free at last, his muscular body leaped out and ran toward the open gate, into the wide-open green pasture, running at full speed. It was clear he wasn't going to stop, even at the end. He slid before hitting the fence and falling sideways, but quickly leaped up. I sunk down and breathed a sigh of relief, knowing my dream was our horse's salvation. He would be fine...

CHAPTER SIXTEEN

THE EVENING NEWS

Come spring, it was time once again to secure stalls. It is one of the most difficult times of the year for trainers. There can be up to twice as many horses as there are available stalls. Complaints are common and the position of track managers difficult.

When horses fail to get stalls, they go to training tracks, which can be as far as fifty miles away. In recent years, because of high demands for this service, several training tracks have sprung up within a twenty-mile radius. Fortunately, we got a stall and the year was off to a good start.

Dusty liked training Glory. He said trainers look for sturdy framed horses. Their strong legs make for fewer problems. Glory was never sick, and, with exception of the ankle injury, rarely needed extra attention. Later, we would find his lack of weight gain was an advantage rather than a deficit.

"I've entered him this weekend," telephoned Dusty one morning.

We were excited about the new season. There is nothing quite like the din of racing fans enjoying the thrill only thoroughbreds can give. I was busy meeting new people and sharing my vision. Unfortunately, Glory's first race went poorly. He lagged behind most of the way and finished at the back of the pack.

The next several races were a continuation of his first performance. As the months flew by, our money dwindled to almost nothing. This unfamiliar lack haunted us. Complaining or worrying did no good. Finally, I went on my knees and prayed very hard. Dusty called shortly afterwards and said he entered Glory in a race that looked promising. The class was the same we had been running, the lowest, but the entrants to this race were like us, losers.

"I'm sorry Renee, but I couldn't get him in the race. There were too many entries. But I did get him in this one."

We were disappointed. Our horse would be competing in a mile race with horses far superior to him, including Jake's best horse! We knew it was hopeless but steadily growing in the knowledge of the racing business.

Off the phone, I hurried to a nearby drug store and picked up a racing form.

Scanning the tenth race told me Glory would definitely be a long shot...a very long shot! Jake's horse was the favorite.

There were raised eyebrows with Rich and out other owners. However, we were satisfied that Dusty thought Glory was good enough to keep him racing. His hock had not swollen up after a previous race. That was a positive sign, though one cannot bank how long or if it would hold up. Strangely enough, we didn't worry about leg problems or cared if he ran well or not. It was just the pleasure of enjoying the sport of kings!

The day of the race was hot and muggy, unusual for our part of the country. The horses were sweating before they ever reached the front stretch. So were we. Glory had pulled post position four. Jake's horse, Darnani, was the racing form favorite, drawing post position ten. As Jake passed us, I hid my face. It was hard to forget his sneer when we tried to enter the race, a look that blared "what the heck are you doing trying to put Glory in this one!"

I shot a glance at the tote board. Glory was forty to one.

"These are the exacta payoffs," said the announcer.

The exacta is a special ticket where you have to pick the winner and second place horse in the race, in that order.

The announcer spoke again. "Number four, For His Glory' $2,200."

It was no wonder Jake mocked us. We still put six dollars across the board, just in case. At 40 to 1, even show (third place money) would give us our money back.

"And they're off!" cried the announcer.

Glory leaped high out of the gate and settled into eighth place on the first turn of the mile and a sixteenth race. To our amazement, he gradually passed several horses. Toward the homestretch, he passed two horses, which put him in fifth place. Four horses, including Jake's Darnani ran neck and neck, all vying for the win.

Because of the impossible odds, my usual nervousness at the beginning of a race did not manifest. Now I was in hard labor, my rapid heartbeat unstoppable. Is this really happening? Was the impossible about to happen again?

"For His Glory is making a move and is now in third place," proclaimed the announcer as the runners came out of the second turn.

We held our breath, wondering if he could hold up the pace. Rich, who held my hand since the gate opened squeezed it tighter, each looking at one another, sensing each other's heartbeat.

Then came the stretch run, the most exciting part of racing. We yelled our heads off as Glory sailed past the third-place runner. Only Jake's horse was in front of victory land.

"And For His Glory is moving up on the rail, Darnani trying to hold on...” shouted the announcer.

At that moment, I saw Jesus riding Glory. I closed my eyes and did a double take. My heart leapt. That is my God out there. He loves riding horses like me...Incredible! Unbelievable! But I saw it. He graced me with His glory of seeing Him. I will never forget that day and that experience!

"It's all For His Glory!" boomed the announcer.

Rich was ecstatic! "Did you see that sudden burst of speed, when he shot forward, past Darnani and won by two lengths?"

I couldn't speak as he wrapped his arms around me, still incredulous of my experience. We held our breaths and raced toward the winner's circle, waiting for the ruling that our horse had truly won. Our group was crying and hugging each other. Consternation paled Jake's face.

The announcer spoke. "The results have now been declared official. In first place is number four, 'For His Glory,' second is Darnani......... "

Elated beyond measure, we walked into the winner's circle. We even invited some friends to pose for the winning photo. I looked at Glory, his eyes blazing, his body heaving after the incredible effort.

“You did wonderful big boy, you did wonderful,” I said aloud as tears cascaded down my cheeks.

“Yes, you sure did, Glory,” said my husband and the other owners.

I looked up into the sky, thanking our heavenly Father for His unmerited favor.

"Great ride!" we all said to our new jockey, Mark Mattell. He smiled and jumped off Glory. The few souls who did bet on Glory still whooped and hollered, congratulating Mark as he walked off. Unbelievably, our little six dollars across the board paid over a hundred dollars!

"Smile," said the photographer.

The announcer again spoke. "For His Glory is owned by Revelation Six Two Stable and is trained by Dusty Liken. Exacta payoff for the first and second place winners of the tenth race, For His Glory and Darnani is $2,159."

After the photographer's official photo, friends stopped us as we exited the winner's circle. One said, 'You should have heard Jake muttering about how ridiculous it was that Glory beat his horse."

Just the day before, Dusty had asked for his day money. All I could say was, "We don't have it," and we did not. Today, the purse money for the win would provide for the expenses of the next three months. What a relief and an incredible blessing!

Friends stopped us as we exited the winner's circle. One said, "You should have heard Jake muttering about how ridiculous it was that Glory beat his horse." From that day, Jake's respect for us gradually increased.

After the race, we joined our group and dined at a nearby restaurant frequented by racetrack enthusiasts. We celebrated with prime rib, my favorite. The camaraderie was heartwarming and a few people even recognized us.

On the way home, we picked up our daughters from my parents' house. "Tell us about the race again," begged our youngest. "We never got tired of telling the story!"

Once home, I fed Iradelle, our huge black and white cat. Then my husband and I lounged on the sofa, waiting for the evening news. At the end of the program is the sports review. We always looked forward to racing news, dreaming how special it would be to win a feature race. Television usually featured clips of the daily double or the feature race.

Suddenly, the announcer beamed widely and said, "Now if you had a $2 exacta ticket on For His Glory at this afternoon's races, you would probably be dancing down the street! The payoff was $2,200, the fifth highest ever paid!"

I almost fell off the sofa! My husband shook his head in disbelief. What an awesome move of God! He had made our little horse known to the public.

One of the pari-mutuel workers, a woman, said she even looked up our stable name in the bible! Yes, God had indeed come to visit the racetrack and He wanted everyone else to know it too!

The following week, I applied for a special car license plate. There was great joy when it was approved! Anyone following my shiny maroon car would see 4HSGLORY. What a conversation starter that became!

"Thanks. What a race!" said Dusty the following morning.

He was grateful for his day money and of course the bonus from placing in the race. We blessed the help too. Glory's win was a much-needed boost for the barn. Everyone had worked doubly hard trying to get a winner. Especially excited was Glory's exercise boy, a tall sandy haired young man named Donnie. He had been having a particularly rough time with his mounts. Glory's win helped Donnie to believe God loves and understands those in his profession.

Another episode in the life of For His Glory had ended on a high note. On the horizon, though, was a stirring, a harbinger of God's purpose at the race track.

CHAPTER SEVENTEEN

FORGIVENESS AND DESTINY

Three years had flown by with life lived in the fast lane. No longer novices, we had seen Glory broken, trained, and raced. We thought we knew the ropes and we did. Yet, unbeknownst to us, up the pike was a rendezvous with fate.

Charles and Danielle Stephens lived on a plateau several miles east of the racetrack. Evergreens surrounded the well-manicured ten-acre storybook ranch. Six-foot whitewashed fences housed mares and frolicking weanlings. A pricey black stallion pranced around the stud corral. It was our fourth season in thoroughbred racing and we had found a new place to board Glory.

"Welcome to Highlight Farm," said Charles, a tall handsome man in his thirties.

"We've heard a lot of good things about your ranch," replied my husband.

"Here comes Danielle. She will show you around. I apologize for leaving so abruptly but I am taking a shipment of horses south. We feel we can help your horse-- even put some weight on him."

"Good to see you again! I would have been here sooner but our four children required some immediate attention."

I had admired Danielle from afar. A tall petite blonde woman with an incredibly infectious smile, Danielle stood out in the crowd. She usually stood at her trainer husband's side at the track, he being considered one of the finest trainers at the track. He owned or held partnership in horses that had won or placed in major stakes races.

Danielle pointed toward the barn. "I want you to meet Miguel, the best caretaker we've ever had. He can solve any problem having to do with horses. Honest, this boy is unbelievable!"

I marveled how Danielle managed to be a dutiful wife, mother of four, run a large ranch for a husband who was often out of town, be at the track for races, and remain sane! An exercise rider when she married Charles, she understood every facet of racing. Danielle was like several women I met in the industry, high energy people who function well under stress. Danielle loved horses and she knew racing!

"Si, it is good to meet you," replied Miguel after introductions.

Danielle's eyes twinkled. "Miguel will take good care of Glory. He says he already knows how to put some weight on him,"

"Yes maam, I do well for him. You will all see."

A thought vaguely crossed my mind. Was it necessary that Glory gain weight? After all, he had run quite well with a skinny body.

We turned to see Glory's van pull in as Charles pulled out of the driveway. Miguel helped unload him as we watched. Glory looked very lean.

"Senorita, he is way too skinny. I fatten him up. You will see!"

Miguel exuded confidence so it was not difficult to trust him, especially because of the reputation of the farm. A special regimen for Glory would start immediately. Miguel would personally prepare Glory's food. If we visited, late afternoons was suggested.

Two very busy weeks passed before I made it out to the Stephens. No one seemed to be around so I moseyed through the shed row, taking stock of who occupied the stalls. Glory was not there so I walked around the building. He was in a small arena, jumping, kicking and sweating profusely. That was not like him. I wondered about the pressure on his ankles from the extreme exertion.

Walking toward the back of the barn afterwards revealed our caretaker. "How's Glory doing, Miguel?"

"Oh, he's starting to put on weight already. Just watch and see how good he'll look!"

"But he's kind of wild out there, sweating too," I replied.

"Just getting out the energy," laughed Miguel.

What could I say? What did I know? For several weeks, this went on. Always Glory was racing around the arena. I surmised it was something Miguel had put in his oats.

Racing season was fast approaching and PR people busy as bees. Hanging plush pink and orange geranium baskets were scattered throughout the track.

The infield was arrayed with thousands of baby annuals. Beauty was everywhere! An aura of optimism filled the air. Of course, our hopes peaked too. Would Glory be even better this year? This week, they would ship him to the track.

My husband got off work early so we could see Glory load for the track. When we got to the ranch to see him loaded, grim faces awaited us. Glory had bowed a tendon, bad news for any horse owner. I pressed the issue of overeating to make him look good, straining to make sense of the calamity. The ranch was clearly at fault but trifled the issue. Somehow, we did not feel right about pursuing it.

A quick call to our other owners showed disappointment and unbelief. Bowed tendons are bad injuries and usually curtail any serious thought of racing again.

It was about this time that Marnie come into my life. We met outside the rail at the half-mile pole of the racetrack infield. She had begged me to let her train Glory.

"Water therapy might help," she suggested. "There is always the chance that enough exercise without pressure on the legs would strengthen a horse and maybe even allow him to run again. I know a prominent whose farm is about fifty miles away."

We and our partners agreed to take the chance, knowing there was no guarantee.

Marnie picked up Glory and trailered him to Doc Fences. We couldn't bear the pain so didn't see him off. It was two weeks before we heard word about his progress.

"I'll meet you down at Doc Fences tomorrow," said Marnie as I visited her barn one Friday morning.

"How's Glory doing?" I asked.

"He's loving the water and his ankle swelling is definitely going down."

Early the next morning, we hustled the rest of our owners and carpooled south. The air was crisp but soon the spring sun popped out between fluffy white clouds, brightening the landscape and our mood.

Dr. Fences' farm was awesome, a pastoral scene fit for a movie. A handsome man in his late fifties, he had a gentle way that invited respect from horses and men.

"We think he's coming along well, considering the extent of his injury," said the vet. "He loves the water and certainly has spirit!"

"How long do you think it will take before he might be able to run?" asked one of our owners.

Doc raised his eyebrow, looked at the ground and back at each of us. "It's probably going to take some time," he cautioned. "Bowed tendons are difficult but sometimes we can bring a horse back. It depends on the injury."

Thankfully, our balloons of hope did not burst. Any hint of recovery potential was enough to motivate us. We had the privilege of enjoying the fruits of our labor many times the last few years. Why give up, yet?

The season was well under way when Marnie called.

"Glory is ready to ship to the track. He's ready and antsy to run," she said with rapt enthusiasm.

Excitement prevailed as we hoofed off once more on a steady basis to the big oval. Marnie's kind, gentle manner and experience with horses made us comfortable. We had been through a lot and there was a peace about being with her we hadn't experienced before. Harder to deal with was pushing away the nagging thoughts...why couldn't we have met sooner?...if Miguel just hadn't been in the picture?

Regret produces more regret so we pushed on, believing everything was for a reason, that there was a bigger picture.

As the weeks went by Glory's heavy body slimmed down, though nowhere near his once skinny frame. He was beautiful and a mature five year old, but would he be able to run again?

"He'll work Monday. Be here at 8:30am," said Marnie one Saturday morning. "Wednesday's card looks good for him. I doubt if there will be many entries. It should be an easy race for him if the ankle stays together."

Everyone showed up for the workout even though it was a weekday. Hopes for a winner resurfaced. It's every horseman's dream. I knew chances were slim but hope rekindled is a flame for the spirit, and my spirit needed a boost.

We all needed a boost, mainly justification for the enormous bills associated with Glory's comeback!

By Wednesday, we nervously awaited the race, hoping for a runner. The fifth race drew nine horses. Glory was post position number eight. That was good. He liked to run on the outside where there was less chance of a mishap. Unfortunately, knowing your horse has a weak ankle can numb your brain. Rather than enjoying the race, I focused on Glory's condition and if he would hold up. It was agony for me. Turns out our group, including my husband, suffered the same fate. Anxiety replaced hopeful anticipation and the only thought was 'will he make it?'.

Glory broke well from the gate and ran at the back of the pack. At the quarter pole, he moved up but not enough to nab fifth place. He finished sixth and appeared as if he came out fine, dancing across the infield with Marnie and a handler.

"The ankle swelled a little bit," said Marnie the next morning when our whole group showed up the track.

Stinging fear erased any thought of a smooth road. Was this an omen, the end?

"What's that mean?" asked my husband as he watched Glory on the walker.

"Well, I'm going to use everything I've learned to bring the swelling down. Don't give up just yet."

Numb, everyone left for home, including my husband. He brought his own car, sensing I needed time alone with my horse and Marnie.

When Glory's time on the walker was over, Marnie walked him back to his stall. Her loving blue gray eyes suddenly met mine. We had become close friends. A woman of faith and incredible horse knowledge, she would be with us through this fire. That's the way I saw it.

Left alone with my Glory, I watched as he circled the stall, looking for just the right position. His large body plopped down and he rolled heavily, enjoying the alleviation of his itching. His legs shot out, precariously close to the edge of the stall. I never ceased to cringe when this happened. Horses can misjudge the space and get cast, a dangerous thing. Inability to get up can actually cause death. That's one of the reasons there needs to be help available anytime day or night in the backstretch.

Glory jumped up, shook off the straw and went to his water. After a drink, he came to me. I rubbed between his ears, what he loved. He laid his head near my chest. I yield to your will, Lord, I said in my heart. Surrender looses one to embrace the future, whatever their destiny.

Our private time over, I navigated the bumpy dirt floor toward Marnie. She was busy measuring oats, salt and bran into feed buckets.

"I don't believe in ruining a horse or putting a jockey in harm's way just because you want day money," she said as I paced the floor.

She had read my mind.

"Give me a little more time, Renee. Another race ought to tell us where we're at."

Her words soothed my spirit. "I trust you, Marnie...okay, we'll try one more."

It was nearly three weeks before Glory ran again. He finished eighth. His ankle blew up again. The end had finally come....and it was okay.

CHAPTER EIGHTEEN

A DREAM COME TRUE

"You just have to meet him," chimed Marnie one mid-summer afternoon.

Her sparkling eyes commanded attention, beckoning once more to meet her 'friend' who lived behind the racetrack.

"Shorty knows more about horses than anyone I've ever met. He is a human horseclopedia. That old man will search until he finds the answer. Besides, his barn is so close to the track. You'll be able to do things with Glory you've never done before!"

Marnie's suggestion was logical…and practical as Glory was now retired from racing and totally mine. I had bought out the other owner shares, a dream come true. Re-breaking him to be my riding horse after his legs healed was an exciting proposition. Though incredibly high strung and a handful, I was optimistic.

Marnie pushed. "The board is cheap compared to other places. I know the barn is not what you are used to by a long shot, but Shorty never fudges on the animals. He's a horse lover."

I finally agreed. "Set me up to meet him and we'll go from there."

Marnie moved quickly. In fact, by late evening she called to schedule an appointment for 7:30 in the morning.

"Wow Mom!" echoed my children as I related the story.

"That's great," smiled my husband with a big hug.

Truly excited about my new venture, they knew my craving to ride Glory was about to materialize. Of course, warnings to be careful dotted their agenda. I assured them I would not try anything too quickly; knowing what strong jockey hands it took to ride the big horse. On the other hand, many ex racehorses calm down once they are retired and the pressure is off them. Naively, I assumed this would be true for Glory.

I awoke the next morning to a ray of sunshine illuminating the edge of our bed. My husband rolled over and kissed me.

I urged him to get some extra winks, knowing he planned to do paper work at home rather than at work. After donning jeans, a tan fringe shirt and blue felt cowgirl hat, I drove to the track. Expectation exploded within my psyche, a new adventure, a new day, the approaching realization of an impossible dream.

Marnie met me as agreed at the track backstretch gate. I jumped into her light blue station wagon and headed for her friend Shorty's house. She chattered the few blocks there. I just listened.

Shorty's quaint little house stood amidst several duplexes dotting thirty acres. I often wondered who owned this prime land right behind the racetrack. I assumed Shorty owned the property, which included a tilted weather-beaten red barn similar to those often depicted in pastoral paintings. A lone scrubby fir tree hugged the right side of the barn. Six feet high, fences circled a small corral, separating it from two pastures.

"Glad to meet you," smiled a pleasant Shorty.

As he reached to shake my hand, I searched his pale blue eyes, set deeply behind a head of curly brown hair. He was clean-shaven and wore a brown plaid shirt and newer jeans. Though in his sixties, he had little grey hair. We were the same height, five foot five. Bowlegged and walking with a slight limp, he reminded me of Jake. It was obvious he had been a cowboy all his life.

I liked him right away. He exuded confidence and his friendly demeanor was magnetic.

Shorty weighed his words then spoke. "You can board your horse here till you make future arrangements. I am mostly into Appaloosas and Arabians. Don't do much with thoroughbreds….not anymore. They're too high strung for me. But as a favor to Marnie…"

He shot a glance at her and awaited my reaction.

My mind was reeling. The price was right and location better than anywhere I've boarded my horses. Besides, Marnie's efforts to secure this meeting endeared our friendship even more.

After a deep breath I looked at Shorty. "We need a place right now. So if you're willing, this would be great."

Before he answers, the front door suddenly opened. It was Marty's son Peter and his girlfriend Joanie.

Handsome Peter had his father's eyes. Several inches taller than Shorty, he was the same height as Joanie, both blonde and blue eyed. After introductions, they disappeared into Peter's room.

"Sit down, sit down," coaxed Shorty as he went to get us a drink.

Marnie watched as Shorty disappeared into the kitchen. "Things will work out real good with him. Besides, maybe you can help him with Peter. The age difference is so great they spar an awful lot. Shorty's wife died real young and he raised his son alone."

"Hmm," I gestured, realizing Shorty had a much younger wife to have had Peter so late in life.

Two glasses of lemonade were set carefully on the coffee table before us. That was not easy since several piles of horse magazines lay there. Shorty caught me glancing at one.

"Learn a lot of things in those magazines. I've collected them all my life," he offered.

I popped the question nagging me for days. "How long do you think it will take for Glory to wind down, I mean for me to be able to do something with him?"

"Every horse is different. Wait until he gets used to these surroundings. I'll watch to see how he's doing."

"I'd appreciate that. Marnie says you've broken a lot of horses, even helped her with her babies on the farm. Glory's awfully nervous and I'm wondering whether he'll calm down."

Shorty rubbed his chin and answered, "Most horses change when they're off the oval but there's always some who never get it out of them, the track I mean."

"I hope Glory is not one of them. I really want to be able to ride him someday."

"Didn't you say you bought your daughter a yearling white Arab?"

"Yes," I answered.

"Well, tell you what? When it's ready to be broken you can bring her here and I'll help much as I can."

I nearly fell off Shorty's sloping couch! Within a month, Pharah Bar Anna, our new venture with an Arabian filly, would be ready to break. As usual, I would be searching for just the right place for her. My prayer was answered before I could even ask it!

Shorty winked at Mary. "I won't charge you much for her because Peter is good with the little ones and I'll let him start the process for experience."

"It's a deal!" I answered.

Marnie was all smiles. I was in shock! There were so many open doors in this one short meeting, more than could ever be expected.

Once home, I piled the experiences of the day on my family. Monica was thrilled. She, like me, was nutsy about horses. Our other daughter's response was precious. Rather than being envious, she encouraged both her sister and me to pursue our expensive hobby.

By month's end, Glory and Monica's filly munched happily in Shorty's lush green fields. They romped around their huge pastures, twice the size of those we had boarded previously. Daily visits to the farm were the highlight of my day. Waiting for Monica to return from school tested my patience, a virtue much needed. Mornings at horse farms bustle with activity while afternoon tend to be quiet and uneventful. I definitely preferred the buzz of mornings. This was definitely a change of pace.

"Let's go! called Monica one mid-afternoon.

"If I can get my boots on," I moaned.

The perfect autumn day had lured me outdoors. My blistered fingers screamed at the slightest pressure. Who would not be exhausted...raking...pulling weeds...moving rocks? Yes, overworking was a habit I had not yet conquered!

"I've got the carrots, Mom," yelled Monica.

With our bags of gold in hand, two horse lovers were soon on their way. Amazingly, we made every green light and got to the farm in record time.

Shorty's truck was nowhere in sight. Neither were the other occupants' vehicles. A lone gray cat streaked across the parking lot, disappearing beneath a broken facial board.

Monica sprinted through the barn to the east fence. She hopped up, hooked her boots on the bottom rung and shouted, "Anna, come get your carrots!"

The filly labored toward us through the dense grass. Monica slowly slipped on a halter as Anna greedily nibbled sweet carrots.

"I'll get Glory now," I mumbled.

He was behind a scrub tree at the far end of the pasture. I forced open the heavily skewed gate. It creaked and groaned. Somehow, Shorty never seemed to get time to fix my minor annoyances.

"Come on Glory!" I whistled.

Glory's ears perked. His majestic head cocked. After a loud neigh and silly crow hop he tore across the field. I loved the sound of those pounding hooves. It was music to my ears, what every horse lover remembers.

Glory skidded to a stop in the soft mud before me. I jumped back as he lunged for a carrot top dangling from my hand.

"Take it easy, big horse," I whispered.

With a subtle move to the side, I slipped on his halter. Thank God for sugar cubes and carrots! Horses do not necessarily like to be 'caught.' Once away, it is tough to coax them back. Frustration mounts each time you are outwitted. Eventually, you feel like an idiot!

Today, the horses were particularly cooperative. As we groomed, Monica and I chatted about our dreams, mostly about how we wanted to enter horse shows.

"There's a 'fitting and showing class' next month at Mayfair Downs," suggested Monica.

"Yes, we'll enter Anna," I agreed.

After combing muddy knotted tails, we stood back and admired our shining steeds.

"This is so exciting, Mom! I always dreamed of showing Arabs, just like Delores.

"They are incredibly beautiful," I replied.

My friend Delores and I had parallel ministries. She was inspired to work in the Arab world though she never had a horse nor desired one. She was my principal encourager in my race ministry. Her first colt made the front cover of Arab World calendar. When Delores and her family moved north that same colt went on to become Alaska State Stud Champion. Rich and I flew there to see the event.

The memory brought tears to my eyes. As I watched Monica, I drank in the joy of precious moments spent between mother and daughter.

Monica and I jumped as a voice resounded behind us.

"Hi," said Peter with a big grin.

"You scared me," I replied

"Sorry."

Anna's ears snapped to attention. She nickered and tried to turn her head but the crossties blocked her.

"She sure knows you!"

"I've been teaching her some basic stuff. She's learning fast," commented Peter as he stroked Anna's neck.

"That's great," I replied. "When will you put a saddle on her?"

"I'll work on it early next week since she's lunging and doing everything so well."

"That's great," I said enthusiastically.

Peter stuck his hands in his jeans pockets and bit his lip. "Well, have to go now since Dad's coming home with more hay. The first load had a few moldy bales."

We waved as he walked out of the barn. Marnie was right. Friendship on this farm was indeed flourishing. Watching Peter work was more thrilling than we could have imagined. Besides, the laidback lifestyle was perfect. I was content being a stay at home Mom and working with horses. Who needed racing?

CHAPTER NINETEEN

A NEW STAR - REVELATION WHAT STABLE?

"Hi Renee," phoned Marnie one evening. "How are things going with you?"

"Couldn't be better--Shorty's place is unbelievably peaceful. The horses love it!"

Marnie hesitated. "Are you sitting down?"

"Well no...but I will."

When I plopped onto the nearest barstool, a shiver shot up my spine.

"What's up?" I asked.

"Cy's been looking at a horse..."

My back tensed as I took a deep breath.

"Cy's been watching this gelding at Turf Downs. He's been running poorly this year. If you look back far enough, he's won some high claimers, even ran in allowance company. With my knowledge of fixing legs, Cy thinks he would be a winner. I've worked with the best, you know, learned the secrets of the trade. We need less than five grand apiece. What do you think?"

Marnie's words hit like an earthquake. Physically and mentally, racing was behind me. Learning to ride Glory and breaking Anna was challenging enough.

With a voice barely audible, I stammered, "I'm not sure I ever want to be in racing again. It's been a great adventure but..."

Oblivious to my resistance, Marnie hurried on. "Come on Renee. You know Cy's good. He's always on the lookout for good horseflesh."

Everyone knew Marnie's husband's knack at picking good thoroughbreds. A man of few words, he was sharp as a tack and thorough. Though a self proclaimed atheist and resistant to the gospel. we got along fine, save for him finding my eyes strange. At least that was what Marnie said.

"Come on Renee? This horse ran well in high claimers. Whoever is training him now doesn't know what they're doing. This horse is a sure bet. Cy knows!"

I swallowed hard, praying for wisdom. God, is this You or a temptation? Can I go through ownership again? The ups and downs? The enormous expense? Yes, it is a ministry...and yes, there is still an unfulfilled prophecy...Nevertheless, I thought you might have changed your mind!

"Talk to your husband, Renee, and let me know soon as you can."

Talk to my husband? I moaned. He would surely say 'no'! Working overtime to provide for horses is not a picnic! I even helped by doing yard maintenance for an elderly neighbor. The pay was meager and the work backbreaking! Even my present venture into real estate just paid the bills.

Though I flatly rejected the idea of another race horse, my husband mulled it over and kept badgering me until I finally agreed. Marnie was, of course, delighted!

Cy won the bid on "John's Vision!" phoned Marnie one early morning.

It was off to the races again...a new adventure, a new stable, and partnership with Marnie's family. It was time to set aside the call and privilege of racing 'For His Glory'. Amazingly, I was returning to the world of horsemen and women who had etched a place in my heart.

This would be my third experience with trainers. While Jake broke me in, Dusty helped me through my anxieties. With Marnie, I knew there would be little stress, not the familiar worries about what could or might happen during a racehorse's career. Her knowledge of the sport, her gentleness and faith not only buoyed my spirit but matured me as a person. I had never forgotten Jake's reference to one of his clients who never questioned what he did. The couple had lost several horses through breaking down, sickness, and even death but they never interfered or blamed their trainer. Jake's emotions triggered in me a desire to be one of those 'perfect' owners. I hoped that could be realized with Marnie and our new purchase. What a joy to finally relax, to have a confidence I'd never known.

Marnie took a liking to John's Vision and immediately went to work on his legs. He was a small horse but with a long muscled body and rather unusual head. His favorite pastime was hanging his tongue out of his mouth.

He did this on the walker, when he stood in his stall, or when he was walking to the track from the barn. It made one think he was a little less than smart, but it was just him, and after all, what or who is perfect? Cy said he ran well as a two year old but was injured, which seemed to limit his career.

It was agreed to use the same jockey silks as Glory but the stable name was changed to 'Revelation 19 Stable'. From the beginning, I knew purchasing 'For His Glory' had been the birth of a vision, 'Revelation 6.2 Stable' the middle stage. However, I never imagined that 'John's Vision' would pave the way for the final part of my vision.

And I saw heaven opened, and behold a white horse; and he that sat upon him was called Faithful and True, and in righteousness he doth judge and make war.
And the armies which were in heaven followed him upon white horses, clothed in fine linen, white and clean.

Revelation 19:11,14

Doubts about the ability of John's Vision were quickly dispelled when he won his first race and several afterward. It was always a fun experience to go to the racetrack office where monies are released. One of the secretaries had been fascinated by the stable name and had asked me what Revelation 6.2 meant. I told her it was a bible scripture and she should look it up. She said she knew it was in the bible and later did so. When we got John's Vision, she was familiar with the first scripture and now it would be fun looking up the new one. It made me wonder whether anyone else had taken the time to pursue the meaning of our stable names. It is humbling to know the second coming of Jesus was being prophesied through my horse ministry.

CHAPTER TWENTY

RIDING GLORY - THE IMPOSSIBLE

"Hey, Renee, there's a great farm not far from here. It's the newest facility around with a huge indoor arena. Why don't you take your horses there?" encouraged Emily, an exercise rider at Century Downs and a riding instructor.

A raven haired beauty with hazel eyes and demeanor of I know who I am and I know where I'm going, her incredible ability to handle horses and seemingly to know their minds inspired me. The grueling winter and my aching back from packing water and wading through knee deep mud at Shorty's made me willing to go to work, if necessary. An inspiration that enabled me to get into a business outside the horse field proved lucrative enough to make the move. Ah... to stable Glory and Anna at a farm which would do the work for me so I could just enjoy my horses!

Barely a half an hour from our home, 'Heart Meadow' was a gentleman's ranch that stabled a combination of thoroughbred and classier riding horses. The twenty acre 'equine resort' was situated on the side of a hill, its white fences stretching as far as the eye could see. Several buildings dotted the property, one occupied by stable hands Dominic and Jose.

"You are in good hands, Senorita, and your horses will get the best of care," they assured me.

Both took a quick liking to Glory and did extra things for him and for me. Both coming from religious backgrounds, we could talk freely about our experiences. There was great rejoicing as even our little prayers manifested quickly.

Riding lessons soon offered an opportunity to better know the owners of the farm, Jesse and Kay. They were a handsome couple, very friendly with their clientele, and regular viewers of those taking lessons.

Never having had a riding instructor, I was more than willing to start in a beginner's class. Practical techniques quickly made riding less stressful, fueling my goal to ride Glory further than a trot.

"I can ride your horse if you'd like," offered Emily one lazy Friday afternoon. Our friendship bloomed after my enthusiastic "yes!". She understood my desire and fears and felt she could help break him into a regular riding horse.

Unfortunately, Emily's first ride on Glory was a disaster. The minute she went faster than a trot he started bucking... at least two times around the arena. This was no small arena and he was no easy bucking horse! The last trip around she managed to jump off.

"Maybe I can't ride this one," she suggested. My hopes crumbled as disappointment painted her face.

"I just bought 'Stanley', an ex race horse to re-break for myself. He'll be a great jumper when his legs are fixed." Happy for Emily, I managed a smile.

Surprisingly, Emily didn't give up on Glory. "I figured out a way to contain him," she said the next time we met. "I'll meet you in the morning at nine and we'll try again."

Though a dismal foggy morning, by eight-o-clock I was already on the road, my heart beating excitedly. Squinting and hugging the steering wheel, I slowly drove down the country road, barely able to see the faded center line.

Relieved at making my destination, I pushed back the heavy sliding wooden door, and walked toward Glory, who was three stalls into the aisle way. Seeing me, he nickered, a large carrot at my side likely spurring him to sway from side to side, then shaking his head.

"Now big horse, time for a little warm-up." I said, hoping for a better lunging experience (circling him at the end of a long line). Anxious to get out of his stall, he moved quickly along, my arms and shoulders holding tightly onto his halter.

By this time, everyone at the barn knew my debacle, as I couldn't even lunge Glory without him pulling it out of my hands and running off. After a couple of circling runs, I managed to catch my wild one and walk him a bit before heading back to his stall.

Emily arrived promptly at nine, her large hazel eyes more serious than usual. She was undoubtedly mentally preparing for her assignment.

"Here we go," she saluted after saddling. I opened the gate to the arena and prayed.

It was a hard ride but steeled Emily managed to keep him from bucking most of the time by moving him in circles. Jesse and Kay joined me as I watched from the stands. I shivered, remembering their words the last time we met. "I'm afraid you're going to get hurt. You'd best quit while you're ahead and ALIVE!" said Kay.

"Why don't you sell him and enjoy life before the horse kills you!" reiterated her husband.

Somehow, I knew I couldn't quit, at least not yet. There was still work to do with Jesse. He was not receptive to any God talk though he grew up in my faith. "I have everything I need and want," he said vehemently. Maybe he needed a horse talking to him...reminding me of Jake's response when he yelled "The horse tells me what to do!" It also reminded me of the amazing bible story of Balaam's donkey when it refused to move even though he beat it. Suddenly, the donkey talked and replied to him "Have I been in the habit of treating you this way before?" Then Balaam saw an angel before them, blocking the way because there was danger ahead. I learned that even the most seasoned race trainers eventually realize they're not always the boss.

Satisfied with the ride, Emily dismounted, gave me a thumbs up, and went to groom Stanley.

I cooled Glory down, rubbed behind his ears and whispered sweet nothings while unsaddling. Once outside, I followed Emily as she walked Stanley toward the outfield.

He was a well built gelding, about fifteen two hands with a perfect white star on his forehead. I felt privileged to be privy to this extraordinary woman's love affair with her horse. Her long black ponytail sailed in the wind as they walked into daisy laden fields and played like children. He would jump as she approached him, then turn around as if to run off. Instead, his tail would swish up and he would go behind her only to catch her attention and snicker as if to say more! more! It was Emily who kept my hope alive for my miracle. Her connection to 'Stanley' went beyond anything I'd ever seen in the horse world. The two were inseparable. Though life revolved around horses for Emily, she dated, enjoyed friends, even aspired to go to college. Emily understood my heart's desire...she had it in Stanley.

The day finally arrived when Monica's Anna was tailored to Heart Meadows. Our once small yearling was now a hand taller and its palomino color gleamed.

"Maybe when you can ride Glory, we can ride together, she said excitedly."

"Would that be special!" I replied.

Mother and daughter were soon enjoying the wonders of an outdoor and indoor arena when an unusual thought invaded my mind.

It involved doing a certain action when Glory started bucking.

Anxious to try it out, I hurried to the arena the following day. Riding at a slow trot at the southwest corner, he immediately started bucking. Thankfully, I was able to stay on till he stopped. Horrified onlookers shook their heads. I tried again and again, thanking God I could stay on. Then came the time to do what came to me the night before.

Before we could turn the corner where he'd usually start bucking, I pulled on the bit with all my might, yanking back as hard as I could, using every muscle in my body to hold him in check. This was my moment of glory, using a divine inspiration to calm the beast. He didn't buck!!

It was an incredible moment of surrender of For His Glory's instinctive response. We continued uneventfully around the arena several times, much to the amazement of onlookers.

Shocked yet not, I knew I was given a gift, respecting the powerful equine beneath my English saddle, yet being in control. I sob as I write these words, caught in a moment of time long past but still etched in my soul. Riding For His Glory...the impossible dream...his and my destiny.

After that experience, we began formal lessons with Emily. Eventually, I was able keep Glory to a trot, an extended trot and even a slow gallop, much to the amazement of everyone including Jesse and Kay.

"His extended trot is phenomenal," raved Emily. "We need to enter the big horse into competition."

I was willing but after my first few shows, I knew Glory was too much for me. I was able to get him to an extended trot but not able to control him in the gallop.

"Don't worry," said Emily. I know Glory's potential and if you agree I'll pay the fees and ride him in the Northwest finale."

"Wow! Are you kidding," I responded. " Only Arabs have won that event.

"If I can keep Glory contained when they ask for a full gallop, I think he can win it," she said confidently.

"Then let's go for it. My family and friends will pray hard. "

CHAPTER TWENTY-ONE

ANOTHER WORLD

Emily continued to work with Glory throughout the winter months. Her efforts paid off as he settled down and I was finally able to ride him in the outdoor ring. As spring approached, we aimed for a show where she would ride.

"Let's go beyond the usual schooling show and enter him in "B" competition," she said one morning after her usual workout. "There are three English classes that would suit him. The stakes will be tough as there are few if any amateurs registered. Most participants are older people who have ridden for years and trainers with very expensive horses."

"Okay. I'll make arrangements and pay the fees," I said eagerly.

It was finally show day, one o'clock on a warm Saturday afternoon. Ranch hands Dominic and Jose hooked up the horse trailer while Emily and I packed the cab with horse gear and her outfit. Glory was somewhat reluctant to enter the two horse vehicle but finally jumped onto ramp and settled inside. Once shut, Emily got in the driver's seat and we were on our way.

An hour later, under a bright blue sky, we pulled into Evergreen Haven, a beautiful outdoor facility surrounded by woods and trails. Horse fanciers were familiar with the upscale center but I never imagined having a horse good enough to compete there.

Glory easily unloaded and was saddled. I walked him until Emily finished dressing, finally adjusting her helmet. Ahead was the entrance table where reservations were confirmed.

"Hey Renee," My first class is in twenty minutes...need to work Glory in the warm-up arena so he can unwind."

Lifting my hands toward them, I proclaimed "Lord, bless them in their endeavors."

As they trotted away I scanned the stands for a good seat. A class in progress helped identify which horses would likely be our competition.

My heart leapt when Glory's first class was announced. Because of his size he was easy to spot in the middle of a pack of about fifteen horses, many

Arabs. Emily quickly spotted me and nodded. I didn't expect much so was not concerned whether he got a ribbon or not.

It was just thrilling to be part of a top show.

With each class, however, Glory improved, but no ribbons.

Thinking this was the end of his debut, I was about to leave when Emily turned and said, "I want to take him in the finale and I'd like to pay the entry fee for it,"

"Wow" I said, surprised by her confidence and desire to enter the most prestigious event of the day.

She sprinted off to register and get the number sheet put on her back, the way judges distinguish horse and rider.

There was a deep sense of fulfillment as memories of my horse journey surfaced...the demands of riding English (my heart's desire), proper grooming for your animal, outfits and helmets for yourself, perfecting the gaits required in competition, the finesse to make transitions look easy. You quickly learn that even perfect performances can go awry when your charge refuses to back up or does so improperly in front of the judge at the end of the ride, thereby losing its prize.

"What's that!" I said aloud when a sudden breeze and rustling leaves spooked a horse behind the arena. Its rider quickly got control and disciplined her mount. If this happened during competition, riders would be forced to turn their horse's head slightly, quietly getting their attention to keep them performing. All this had to be done, of course, without the judge seeing them.

By the prized finale, Emily, like the pro she was, regally sat astride her mount. Glory was definitely the tallest and biggest horse in the competition.

"We've rarely seen a thoroughbred beat an Arab in this particular class so don't expect too much." cautioned a couple next to us. With a shrug, my focus turned to Glory.

"Riders, walk your horses," called the announcer.

Emily nodded as she rode by, making a motion that if Glory didn't win that class she was going to protest!

"Riders, trot your horses," called the announcer. All did well in that round.

"Riders, extend the trot," repeated the announcer a second time.

Glory's extended trot certainly made him stand out. He had an incredible stride and just to stay with him while making it look easy was extremely difficult. I watched his precision body, marveled at the sleek coat that only comes after an immense amount of grooming, thanks to Emily's hours of effort.

My eye caught the judge as she turned to look at the number on Emily's back, which meant points for us. Emily had gone all out for this event, to the extent of getting a European hunt coat. Her outfit was perfection and her equipment the best. If Glory could be controlled, we had a great chance to win.

I was revved, watching my horse's every move, scared yet trusting Emily to do the impossible. Undoubtedly, his extension was best of the class.

"Canter your horses," called the announcer.

Glory responded well under Emily's seasoned hands and again the judge noted him.

The moment was fast approaching, my heartbeat increasing, everyone following the action, watching for any horse to act up and be disqualified. A now hushed crowd sat on edge, the moment frozen in time, hearing only the thud of horses' hooves on the soft soil.

"Riders, go from the canter to a hand gallop," yelled the caller.

All watched anxiously as riders pitched forward to give their horses more head. This maneuver took the horse out of the controlled canter, in other words, put in a jockey position.

My mind reeled to the many times Glory took off and I would lose control, or when Emily rode and she had to turn in circles to slow him down. At other times, it meant turning him into the arena guardrail to keep from going beyond the move we were trying to sustain.

Emily not only made Glory look great but her riding skill was obvious to the trained eye. I saw the judge check Emily's number again. Fantastic! Another point for us.

Holding our breaths, we watched as Emily surrendered her hold, allowing Glory to move out. Our eyes shot between horse and judge, watching as she surveyed each animal and rider in the equine circle, all of them traveling faster and faster. My rapidly beating heart nearly stopped when the judge narrowed her view to Glory.

I knew he was ready to go out of control, but at that moment the judge turned towards other horses.

Emily quickly turned Glory to the outside, likely breathing better knowing the judge missed that move.

"All riders halt and go before the judge," called the announcer.

After each horse backed up properly, I saw the gleam in Emily's eyes.

When the judge finished her markings, she handed them to the announcer. "The winners are: fifth, fourth, third, second, and in first place "For His Glory."

I jumped from my seat as the crowd clapped and clapped, even the naysayers next to me. Then came the privilege of seeing a blue ribbon and beautiful plaque presented to Emily.

"Can I keep them? she said as she rode past me.

With tears, I nodded, realizing she had achieved a very special goal. This lovely young lady was really riding for herself rather than for me. This had been the only show where she had paid the fees. It was the pinnacle of her career. Her efforts and love for Glory were rewarded. The impossible had happened to a horse that just about everybody had given up on.

My heart was full of praise and thanksgiving. Yes, Glory, you established a bit of fame, first in racing, then in the show ring. Your regal stance and exquisite body commanded attention. God chose you for unique experiences in this world and to bless those who would help you achieve your highest potential.

Emily's win in the B horseshow opened the door to greater recognition of Glory's talent. Knowing that, however, did not prepare me for what was to transpire.

It began one lazy afternoon after circling Glory around the arena several times. Caught up in the joy of riding, I hadn't noticed two pair of eyes watching our every move. On dismounting, two women approached me.

"Hi. My name is Maureen and this is Nancy."

"Nice to meet you," I replied. "My name is Renee."

"We are very impressed with your horse and would like to ride him. We're dressage trainers."

"Sure," I replied, remembering seeing the pair before.

Nancy mounted Glory and circled the arena with such ease of motion that even I was flabbergasted. The only problem was when she got to a certain corner of the arena (yes, that corner!) he suddenly reared. She quickly got control and steadied him, finishing the ride.

"He has such strength and potential," the women commented. "We'd like to come back tomorrow if that would be okay with you."

"Uh, yes. I'll be here tomorrow, around four."

"Thanks, we'll be there," said Maureen delightedly.

I cringed, wondering how my sometimes-unpredictable horse would fare in one of the most demanding sports for horses. What the women didn't know was Glory had been lunged and ridden quite a while before they got there. It was hard to say if Nancy could have done so well were he fresh out of a stall.

"Now big horse," I said while stroking his head, "you better behave in that corner!"

My big baby threw his head, almost knocking me off balance.

"We'll see about this behavior," I said, smacking him on the side.

I melted as his dark eyes softened and gave me that what? me?' look.

The next day, after lunging, we circled the arena. On the second go around, Glory suddenly reared, catching me off guard, so much so I couldn't bring him down. He sailed across the nearly 60 foot wide expanse, prancing on his hind legs and putting on quite a show for bystanders with shocked faces.

By the grace of God I stayed on but was scared to death to go to that corner again. When I did, the same thing happened. Up till then, it seemed like I was forever climbing a mountain to make Glory my riding horse. It was nerve wracking. One minute he could be so sweet and then suddenly turn into a brute beast!

Jesse and his wife walked in and to my horror gave me the look! As I walked Glory out, she waved me over. "I think your horse is too much for you.

We can find a nice one that you can ride that won't be so dangerous. Besides, from what I know, there is not much chance of breaking that rearing habit."

I shook my head in agreement, but stubbornly determined that Glory was not going to get the best of me, not after winning the B show.!

"God, you have to help me again," I said under my breath.

When the dressage trainers arrived that afternoon, I prayed they would not want to ride.

"I'm sorry, but we have an appointment we can't miss. How about tomorrow instead?" said Nancy apologetically.

I swallowed hard and thanked the Almighty.

The next morning, an inspiration regarding the rearing problem came. I couldn't wait to try it out.

"Okay, big horse. You are not going to get the best of me," I said while grooming and picking his hooves.

Gathering my lunge line, I led him to the arena. Pent up energy manifested quickly as he kicked out his hind feet several times. After bridling and saddling, I mounted my steed, trotted and cantered him toward the far left corner of the arena.

With a boldness and discernment rarely experienced, I sensed Glory's body stiffening, ready to pull another fast one on me. At that moment, I pulled down on the reins, tight as I could, pulling his head down with all my might. He tried to get away from my strong hands but each time I pulled harder. Finally, he stopped fighting me. After a few more tries, we circled the arena without mishap.

An extraordinary inner confidence and peace came over me, a humble knowing I had reached the pinnacle of riding experience. Yes, again conquering the impossible... with Divine guidance.

Now confident that Maureen and Nancy would have a decent ride, I looked forward to their coming that afternoon.

"He's really an amazing horse with that extension," they both proclaimed after their ride.

I was elated!

"We would like to give you an offer to purchase. This horse could go all the way to nationals. We have to own him, though, in order to go through all the pain, it takes to get to the top."

"I'll consider it," I replied numbly.

As I unsaddled him, my mind reeled, my insides feeling like they were tearing apart. Recollection of past experiences of having to let my 'baby' go droned on and on, like a movie reel that wouldn't stop.

I had considered leasing as an option but never faced the idea of selling. The thought of possibly never seeing Glory again was inconceivable!

Then came an inner prompting, pointing out that I had become too attached to my four legged friend, not regarding the desire and purpose of the One who had given him to me in the first place. Finally yielding to what I knew was best for Glory's future, I agreed to sell.

Nevertheless, I cried for days and kept asking God 'why?'

A contract was eventually written and signed by all parties. There was a stipulation that for a four week period, the trainers would work with him. They wanted to make sure he could perform as they wanted to take him to the top of the show circuit. I was confident everything would be okay.

The day arrived for the physical transfer. It was cloudy and gloomy, much like how I felt. As Glory's trailer pulled away, I leaned against the barn, weeping in my humanity. Loneliness gripped me as a leech. Oh, woman of supposedly great faith, you are a mess, I thought.

In the midst of this agony, I received another vision of a happening in the future. There in my grief was the faithful hand of the Almighty, giving me a preview of something that had the potential to be greater than anything I could have imagined. Immediately, the void in my heart was filled with the knowledge there is always another scene in one's walk with God. One vision was ending but there was a rainbow on the horizon. Yes, God the Creator is always creating something new... for His glory.

CHAPTER TWENTY-TWO

PEOPLE– ALMOST A SOAP OPERA

As my life intersected with many people, so did opportunities to be a blessing or bring a word of caution in their lives. These are a few of their stories.

LOLA

I walked toward a new stable, one occupied by a trainer with a national reputation. No one seemed to be around so I started to walk away. Suddenly, a loud moan erupted from the feed room I had just passed. A dark haired woman, seemingly in her mid twenties, was sitting atop a bale of hay. Her elbows rested on dirty wrinkled jeans and her head was cupped between ruddy hands.

"Are you okay?" I said gently.

She tilted her head, tears and mascara oozing down her olive skinned face. "No. My head aches something furious. This mare knocked the side of my head. Who are you?"

"My name's Renee. A friend told me about this barn and I just came to check it out."

"My name's Lola. She pointed across the shed row. "I slept in that stall last night. He's my favorite stallion and I had no place to go. Oh, this headache!!"

I looked deep into Lola's big black eyes. Hopelessness framed them like smothering tentacles. Yes, there was much more than a headache behind those eyes.

"I had no one to turn to, nowhere to go," she moaned.

I groped for my trusty aspirin case and gave Lola a couple.

"Thank you," she said and went to find her water bottle.

Afterwards, we sat down and she poured out her story. The previous day, an uncooperative mare hit the right side of her head and knocked her against the stall wall. The door to the stall was slightly ajar and only a quick reflex on Lola's part kept the animal from escaping. The effort, however, was too much for her body and she shrank down to the straw and lay there quite a while before help came.

"The mare quieted down but I had to deal with my hatred for it," she said. "I've had enough experience to know that bumps and bruises from hot blooded race horses are inevitable. But this horse is real mean! I've catalogued her and she's one to stay from as much as possible!"

I sat still, unable to grasp Lola's circumstances. She had almost no money and her paycheck wouldn't come for another week. I had to do something.

"You need to come and rest for a few days at my house, okay?"

Lola's black eyes doubled in size. "You'd invite me to your house. You don't even know me!"

"Yes."

Lola looked down at the cement floor. "I need to get better. I'll come if you really want me to."

"Good. Get your things and I'll come back after you talk to your boss."

She slowly got up and pointed toward the north end of the barn. "Speaking about Barney, there he is."

The nationally known trainer I'd heard so much about walked toward us and introduced himself.

We shook hands. "My name is Renee. My friend worked for you and told me to come see your barn. Then I met Lola."

After hearing her story, he replied "You get a few days rest. I'll have someone take over until you're well."

Lola managed a slight smile.

"He's a good trainer and real nice," she said as he walked away.

I brought Lola home to my family that afternoon. They totally accepted her. Our oldest daughter even gave up her bedroom. Lola was our family's first intimate exposure to a homeless person. Homelessness was no longer just a word around our home but a human being whose needs we were trying to meet.

I tucked the young woman in bed. She slept that night and most of the next day. Though groggy upon waking, she kept saying how grateful she was for the opportunity to get well.

But then began a daily litany of reasons why Lola thought I could help some of her friends. I wondered who these friends were?

Praying for Lola's head injury to be healed was a strong priority. From then on, prayer, nourishing meals and heaps of encouragement were her daily medicine. Each day she grew a little stronger.

One night Lola grasped my arm tightly. "They're prostitutes' downtown. I know you can help them!"

This petition was more than I could handle. In fact, I freaked out! Where had Lola been? What kind of life had she led? Did she have any family? My mind was barraged with questions.

Not wanting to shake her faith, I stammered, "That's an unfamiliar area to me but I promise to pray about it."

Lola tried to understand. But how could she? I had lived a very sheltered life. When an inner voice said "no," I knew I would not be helping Lola's old friends.

It was a quiet afternoon, the girls gone out with their dad. Lola began to tell me about her life, how she was separated from her husband and their two young children. I was shocked. Even more surprising was the knowledge she had once won a bronze medal in the Olympics. Lola had traveled much and known the good life. But then came a downward spiral of drug abuse. Finally, her husband took their young boys and left. My mind was spinning. Lola's life story could be a book!

After nearly a week in our home, this child of God finally felt well enough to go back to her grooming job at the track.

A short time later I met Lola's ex-husband. He seemed stable and a good father to their children. We talked a lot in the following weeks. Finally, he and Lola got back together. They remarried and had another child. I worried, however, if she could sustain her newfound peace and conversion as she had no church affiliation. For someone with as many problems as Lola had, the transition to a better life needed to be supported by a very strong faith life.

DEENIE

Jake's wife, Deenie, was a slight built woman in her late sixties, often complaining about chronic back and shoulder pain. One day I ventured forth and asked if I could pray for her. Surprisingly, she agreed. I discreetly laid my hands on her shoulders, wondering if the action would be questioned later.

After prayer she continued to sit so I casually walked to the living room and became engrossed in a television show. After several minutes, I realized she was pacing between the kitchen and living room.

"I believe. I believe," she muttered under her breath.

It finally dawned on me that something happened.

"No more pain. I have no more pain, Renee!" Which of us was more surprised is debatable.

"But I saw you take some pills before we prayed," I said cautiously.

"Renee, I've been taking those pills for years and they always take a half hour to work, ALWAYS!

'"Praise God!" I replied with incredulity.

Deenie's radiant face and gesturing hands greeted me the next morning. She was free of pain! This frail woman continued to remind me she prayed each night in front of a picture of Jesus. Her healing not only boosted my faith but I sensed our Creator enjoying the journey with me.

JAY AND JANICE

It was early spring and the ranch buzzed with excitement. Jake's first shipment of horses was ready for their transition to the racetrack. He had arranged for a horse trailer to take For His Glory and a couple of his stable mates to the track.

"This is your big day, Renee," he chided.

I was struck by the unmistakable sparkle in the old trainer's eyes. He'd likely been through this scenario hundreds of times. Yet it was like the first time…anticipation that a horse from your barn might become a big winner.

That spirit accepts the hardships while knowing the privilege of doing what you truly love.

By this time Glory knew me well. I watched every move he made, trying to learn as much as possible about the technical aspects of racing, i.e. proper shoeing and what it takes to keep a horse healthy and fit. Though restricted in handling him, an occasional bunch of fresh grass made our relationship green!

"Can't feed old Glory enough, even after the vet's recommendations," remarked Jake one morning.

I said nothing, knowing his backbones protruded even more after constant work on the exercise track.

Around this time, people began to make a point of telling me Jake was too hard on his horses. Ironically, most everyone acknowledged he was a master at breaking them. The contradiction puzzled me. Did Jake push his animals like he pushed himself?

On the positive end, even with a bony appearance, Glory's exceptional stature drew people's attention, roman head and all. Other owners and visitors often asked about him.

The big day finally arrived. With the necessary paperwork completed, we were okayed to enter the track. Jumping in our car, Rich and I followed Jake's trailer to the Century Downs backstretch gate. A guard waved us through after a proud display of our owners badges. After the season started, Jake said we'd have to park outside. For now, the track was quiet and only a few trainers brought in horses.

A casual glance in my rear view mirror reminded me of Aunt Julia's house; of looking out the parlor window, wishing I could be in Uncle Alex's racehorse world. They were gone as was their house and saloon, torn down for a trailer park for housing backstretch workers. A tinge of sadness eclipsed the joy of the moment.

Passing row of stalls, we came to a stop at Jake's shed row. It was in a prime location, right next to the main entrance to the infield.

Rich ran to open my door, acting like an escort to see the queen's horse arrive. I gushed with pride.

Jake rubbed his chin and pointed down the shed row. "Had this barn over thirty years, you know. I like it here…just a stone's throw to everything…the track, kitchen, and race office. Couldn't ask for better."

A man and woman walked toward us. "Hi Jake."

"Hey. Meet Renee and Rich, 'For His Glory's' owners."

"Glad to meet you. I'm Jay and this is my wife, Janice." Jake excused himself.

"We're excited about taking care of your horse," said the couple who looked likely were in their late twenties. "

I was instantly attracted to Janice, a woman about five feet three with short wavy blond hair. From that day forward, she became a ray of sunshine in a world I was trying to understand.

Jay, a handsome man, about five foot ten, had deep dark eyes. Something about them puzzled me.

The couple showed us where they lived with their two small daughters, all cramped in a tack shack at the end of Jake's shed row. How someone, let alone a family of four, could survive in this small space was and still is a mystery to me. Cleanliness was not their best suit. But, since they scrupulously cared for the horses and were so pleasant, who was I to judge their home?

Likely hearing about Glory from Jake, Janice eagerly addressed me. " I wrote a story about God in high school, but really didn't get much further in my relationship with Him."

"Maybe we can talk about that sometime," I suggested.

Jay offered, "I'm agnostic though I grew up Catholic…began to delve in eastern religions. Yeah, I was disgusted with changes in the traditional church and not being able to identify with any spirituality left me in limbo."

I saw that Jay's darkness was a loss of faith and the human search for meaning to life. My road was cut out. Two precious children of God needing a little direction in their lives.

The couple proceeded to give us a tour of the thirteen horses in Jake's stable, seven being taken care of by Jay and Janice, the others by another groom.

"This is Ron," said Jay, as a young man walked toward us. "He'll care of Glory when we're not here."

"Good to meet you," we said.

"Let's unload your horse and show him his new home," said Jay.

The three walked to the van, carefully coaxing him out. Glory was all eyes, surveying his new surroundings.

Once in the stall, he circled it several times. Finally, his huge neck peered out at the horses down the shed row. A loud whinny sent us backwards, a few drops of saliva hitting us.

"Time to go," said Rich as he wiped his jaw.

I grinned. Jay and Janice smirked as they waved goodbye to tend other horses.

Rich grabbed my hand as we went to celebrate our first experience in the backstretch restaurant. The sights, sounds, and good food meant a lot of meals there in the future. Paying for our meal, we recognized the cashier as the mother of kids who went to school with ours.

"So good to see you, both. she said. "Do you know my son is going to be a jockey?"

"Now, that's exciting!" I said.

Ironically, one of the first visitors to visit Glory was my Pastor. He later told me he had an interesting conversation with Jay. On the other hand, another minister friend was not open to my vision at the track, said I was going to hell and should stay in the church where it's safe. I assured him all was well and time would reveal the fruit of true vision.

As the weeks passed, an amazing thing happened. It was Jay and Janice's day off. I overheard Ron say that Glory was the best horse to take care of in the barn. Thinking my ears mistaken, I went over and asked him to repeat his statement. It was true.

Could the transition to the racetrack, the Pastor's or our prayers, effect a horse that became sweet to handle? After all, no one wanted to work with him at Jake's ranch.

Riding our horse was another matter. He was a ball of lightning and only a handful of people could ride him. Since mornings seemed to be his specialty, Jake's constant reference to him as 'morning Glory' hurt. That's because energy in the morning does not necessarily manifest at actual races. Soon he was calling 'our baby' old bones and then feeding him more to try and save face.

As time went on, I began to realize the magnitude of abuse involved in trying to get two year olds to the racetrack. Glory was broken and learning to race before he even reached two years old. For an extra large gelding like him, it might have been better to wait longer, till he was fully developed and grown. Yet who knows whether he would have been less nervous and filled out physically?

There are also economic and management pressures that force equines to a life of regimentation before they are ready physically or mentally. Yes, mentally too.

Though blame is often charged to owners wanting their horses to race as two olds, most owners I encountered were willing to wait rather than push them too early. I realize two-year-old races are here to stay. Trainers do their best to keep the horses together without any debilitating injuries. Those who make it are called lucky.

One day Janice pointed out a particular chestnut horse at the end of our shed row. His handler was little Joe, the gentleman who lived in Jake's tiny house. Sixty years old and a perpetual bachelor, he radiated warmth, cheer, the epitome of one who has learned to fully enjoy the little things in life. Content to remain in the background, he was to become my soothing oasis when the hardness of Jake got the best of me. Being especially courteous to Deenie, I realized he was a stabilizing influence on the farm. Jake said he could trust him with anything, a rare comment from a man who easily found fault with just about anyone or anything.

"This one is special," remarked little John.

One look at this magnificent creature and even a greenhorn could tell he was something special. The owner was offered an enormous amount for the stud but it was rejected. Unfortunately, my first tortuous experience with horses would involve this horse. Within a few months of training, he walked off the track after a morning workout and fell dead in the barn from a heart attack. It was a terrible shock to everyone, especially Jake, who remained silent for quite a few days after the incident. Evidently, it wasn't anyone's fault because the horse just had a bad heart. That taught me how fragile these four legged creatures can be. From this point on I prayed even harder for Glory, that he would be protected and able to race. This prayer would be tested more times than I care to mention.

Jay and Janice began to drill into me harder than ever that Jake put too heavy a burden on his horses, especially two year olds. They even alluded to training Glory themselves as Jay was trying for his trainer's license. They proved right about Jake's horses because by the end of the year only two horses remained in his barn, Glory being one of them.

In all fairness, Jake may have been easier on his horses at the beginning of his career because some were big money winners. He loved to tell me about them and several photos on the wall showed the glory of his heyday.

One day I casually mentioned something about him having a bad day. He turned around with a glaring stare and said, "I never have a bad day!"

I marveled at his toughness though that strength would be challenged by physical problems that developed soon afterward.

The result was a mellowing of his hard nature.

Shockingly to naïve me, I learned that Jay and Janice were not really married. A few years after leaving Jake's barn I ran into Jay. He was a totally different person. He said Janice had left him. Groping for the meaning of life, he happened to meet a lovely girl name Jolene and they married. My greatest joy was hearing he had an experience with the living God. What music to my ears! Maybe something said at Jake's barn, the Pastor, or our prayer eventually yielded good fruit. The haunting look in Jay's eyes had disappeared, replaced by a serenity that astonished those who knew him. I prayed Jan also found peace and fulfillment though I never saw her again.

JOHN AND ELI

It was a lovely spring morning, my back soaking in the warm sun. I wandered through the backstretch searching for just the right barn to visit. Eli's barn seemed to be calling. A gentle man in his mid sixties, Eli trained a few horses, mostly his own. We chatted a bit about the horses in his barn when we were suddenly interrupted.

"This is John," said Eli.

A large muscular man about Eli's age, John sported full jowls, devilish eyes, and an incredible head of thick hair.

"I only train my one horse because of my Pari-mutuel job during races, " said John after introductions.

Eli and John exchanged horse `talk while I listened, pondering the intensity of John's eyes.

After sharing about his previous day's winner and that I had a part in the victory, Eli slipped me a wink.

"It was Divine intervention," I reminded Eli.

"You know, she's right, John. She prayed for my horse. It couldn't have won under any circumstances with its problem and all."

John stared in unbelief, a sneer replacing his previous smile.

Several days previous, a strong urge compelled me to pray for the animal. The filly had an irreversible breathing condition that would prevent her from ever winning a race. Several vets had confirmed the diagnosis. Although belief in prayer and God was a struggle for Eli, he was unable to contest the results for even the veterinarians couldn't humanly explain his horse's win.

After a couple of minutes, John walked off.

"There's something about that man's eyes," I commented to Eli.

"Yes," I admit. They scare me too. I'd be afraid to trust the man.

The next day would be a marathon for me, a strange appointment with destiny. It started when I ran into John. He nearly had to drag me to see his horse. Usually enthusiastic about meeting and getting to know race trackers, I wanted to run this time. My discernment was correct. John tore into me about the existence of God, why there was evil in the world, Christianity was cruel, etc., etc. ad nauseam.

After each accusation, John's voice grew louder and louder. I looked around; sure the whole racetrack was beaming onto this violent one-way tirade. Thankfully, it was close to lunchtime and there weren't many people around.

For one hour it felt like I was being nailed to a whipping post, unable to escape John's continual barrage of questions. Certain ones made me feel I was being spiritually undressed. Yet, I stupidly answered them anyways. After making several excuses to leave, a phenomenal thing happened. It was as though a Divine power within me took over, suddenly filling my mouth with potent words.

After nearly a half hour, John was so assaulted by these words that he not only backed off but walked away. What I wouldn't give for a tape of that conversation! But the words of power and wisdom in response to John's accusations against God, Jesus Christ and Christianity are lost to that half hour. I can remember none of the conversation to this day.

It took barely twenty-four hours to reap the fruit of that experience with John. I expected nothing from the confrontation, only the joy of knowing a power greater than I lifted me up when I was down.

It happened the next day while walking past John's stable. Much to my chagrin, he called me over to him. Talking non-stop and with unbelievable exuberance, he proceeded to tell me that for six months he had searched for the key to his horse's problem.

"God has given me the key!" he exclaimed.

Shocked, I listened as John went on and on about his discovery.

I was absolutely flabbergasted, how this man's life had been touched. Amazing, because he seemed totally unbelieving the day before.

Moreover, the change was manifest in his eyes. A new softness and light shone. A year later, I heard John moved to another track and had won two races. A friend said John might have had a deep hurt that was exposed during 'God's time with him.'

Rarely did a race tracker come to such faith so quickly from so far. For many the road to faith and peace is arduous and many never find it. A merciful God chose to reach down and challenge John, a far better gift than having a winning race horse, though that helps.

I had finished writing the story of John and Eli when I happened to pick up my bible for my nightly reading. It opened to Psalm 19.8 which says "The laws of the Lord are right, rejoicing the heart: The commandment of the Lord is pure, enlightening the eyes."

Surely this man and his horse came out of darkness into the light. The eyes certainly reveal much....

MARV

One sunny morning when I was attending Glory, a tall, dark haired man rushed by me. I thought he looked familiar but couldn't place why. After a second and third appearance, we began a conversation. Voila! We had gone to the same high school.

Reminiscing about the old days and each other's lives, I found Marv in an unusual situation. He was married to a woman who was the basic breadwinner. Since he had done poor financially, they lived off her programming wages. I wondered about that since he was very articulate and appeared more cultured than most in the backstretch.

"Jake is my father," he said.

Shocked, I was afraid to pursue the subject since Deenie and Jake were supposedly childless.

A few days later, Marv provided the fuel for my growing urge to ride a thoroughbred.

"You can ride my pony horse," he offered.

The horse was pasturing at Jake's with the intention to be used later at the track. Unfortunately for me, Marv failed to say the horse hadn't been ridden for over a month. The ride was a joke, taking an hour for me to get him to stay at a walk.

Some of the problem was my own fault and fears. After all, it had been several years since I'd ridden horses.

Marv was wonderfully patient but in the end conceded I needed a lot more practice to be able to gallop a racehorse, my secret ambition. The thrill of riding again had returned with a vengeance.

Sharing with others about Marv, my newfound friend, proved costly. His reputation was mostly negative. People referred to him as thief, cheater, violator of track rules, a loser and an unstable character in the horse world. The irony was that he had a college background, unusual in the field of racing. Obviously, character education was of little benefit to Marv. I pondered why.

Eventually, someone told me his story. His mother had a relationship with Jake and became pregnant. He offered to marry her but she refused and married another man. Jake's background was not revealed to him. He supposed his mother's husband was his father. One day at the track, someone told him he looked like Jake's kid. He pursued the accusation and found it to be true, verified by his mother. That started an on again off again relationship with his father. He and Jake sparred, often causing Marv to disappear for a time, only to come back and the relationship begin once again. He told me he had nothing to do with horses before meeting his birth father. After that, he couldn't stay away from them. It was latent in his genes!

Confusion in Marv's mind seemed to block any real chance of conversion. He was pleasant yet immovable. Both he and his Dad had problems with character though Jake hid his better.

One day, after morning workouts, Marv cornered me. "What's this thing about God, anyway? It's in the papers everyday!"

I grinned. Splattered throughout our town's newspapers that week was a well-known football sports figure getting national recognition. His faith life was unmistakably given as the reason for his success.

Marv couldn't understand this kind of acknowledgment. One thing I learned at the track was that when things were going well, God was relegated to the background. One felt little need to assess their life and eternal future.

Sadly, Marv's wife filed for divorce and they separated. The loss in his life coupled with the death of his mother created a huge void in his life.

Perhaps that enabled him to consider God. "I'll think about what you've said," he told me one day.

Greatly comforted by that statement, I prayed he would see and walk with his Creator.

MS. BIGSHOT

I was on my way home, driving my trusty old car down the backstretch of the track.

"Pray for that horse," said an inner voice.

With hands growing clammy and a heart beat likely off the charts, I argued.

Could it be? Why me? I don't even know her, just her reputation!

About seventy feet away stood a woman with two men in front of a stable. They were standing next to a chestnut two year old, whose head was bent over. I knew why.

"But she's a tough woman, Lord, and she'll never believe me!!"

I knew there was no choice. This was a command not a suggestion!

Parking in a nearby lot, I showed my pass to the officer attendant and walked toward the distinguished woman trainer. The area was under heavy security and I wondered how to get her attention, and which words might produce a positive response. Then I would lay hands on the dying animal. I was shaking with human fear and the fear of God.

Suddenly, the woman walked toward me and asked, "Can I help you?"

"I'm being inspired to pray for your horse," I stammered.

"Who do you think…. (Expletives)…you are!!

It was useless. She was closed-minded and angry. I walked back to the car, visibly shaking and sad. I doubted the expensive colt would make it. The best vets had been called in with no success. The next morning the horse died. I wondered… if only…

STEPHEN

I met Stephen one morning on my daily walk to the infield track. We stood watching the workouts, commenting on different jockeys. A recent trip to Florida proved unprofitable so he came back to his northwest home and found a job at the racetrack.

I marveled at Stephen's eighteen-year-old ambition and physical prowess. He was ready to attack the world and find his place in it.

Talking about one's eternal destiny was not on his priority list. It was hard to pin him down on anything regarding God. His answer was "why would a woman be talking like you at the racetrack? It's not the likely place for a lady and what about the gambling and such?"

I answered, "I was raised with the idea that you can take your spending money and do whatever you want with it. Thousands of people, including my grandfather, came with little money because they enjoyed the sport. On the other hand, there are compulsive gamblers who lack self-control and should never be there."

Stephen shook his head and wandered off. I didn't see him again till several weeks later. In the meantime, I had been asked by a friend to attend their church conference. While sitting across from three young men, I finally got the courage to ask them if they had a brother.

"Yes," they said incredulously. "But he's hopeless because he's caught up in the racetrack world." What a joy it was to tell them that Stephen was my charge and I regularly challenged him with the gospel.

One of the three remarked, "You must be the woman that he talked about, a woman preacher who had come to his stable."

I sighed, "Yep, that was probably me. I don't think you have to worry about your lost brother. God has his address!"

ELI'S MIRACLE

Rich stepped onto the front porch of our home early one Sunday morning. We were on our way to church. The kids followed him while I made sure the door was locked. An inspiration to go the racetrack suddenly invaded my mind. I looked down at my dress and high heels, then to my family getting in the car. The call was unmistakable. I had to go.

"Honey? Do you mind if I go to the track. I don't know why but I'm supposed to go."

Rich looked deeply into my eyes, surprised but not uneasy.

"I'll take them to church. Do what you need to do."

Thank you God for the gift of such a wonderful husband, I said while ascending stairs to change my clothes.

Rich was my greatest supporter, even to working extra hours to pay expenses.

He was one of the few who understood my calling into mainly a man's world, rarely questioning anything having to do with racing.

Light Sunday morning traffic found me at the track in less than ten minutes.

Shed rows bustled with grooms washing down horses and stalls being cleaned. Horses with their riders clip-clopped down the center road, returning from workouts. The smell of horses was in the air and I loved it!

To be able to be part of the racehorse world, its sights, sounds, lows and highs, was such a privilege. Looking to the sky, I praised the Almighty for His glory.

A quick glance down Eli's shed row did not find him. One of his sons was helping with his stalls.

I ventured in, finding him lying on a cot in his tack room. That was very odd, especially at that time of morning.

"Sorry I haven't been here for quite a while," I said. "Glory's been taking my time with all his quirky problems. You know how that goes?"

Eli laughed and talked about several things. He suddenly grew serious and spoke, "I've had a lot of pain and am going for surgery tomorrow morning."

My mind raced. Would this man, whom I considered the greatest gentleman I'd met in the racehorse world thus far, accept personal prayer? Eli's wife, whom I often saw at church, told me she had prayed for him for thirty years. Racing was in her husband's blood. His family had worked in various facets of the profession for generations. But the men seemed to shy away from religion.

I took a leap of faith. "Do you think I could pray for you?"

Eli's gentle but pained blue eyes looked straight into mine. He hesitated and said, "Yes, you may."

I laid my hands on his shoulder and intense prayer erupted from my lips. I was taken aback at some of the words since Eli had not revealed what his problem was. The prayer over quickly, he thanked me. I walked out of the shed row knowing that was the reason I was supposed to be there that morning.

Try as I may, I couldn't get back to Eli's barn the rest of the week. Something always interfered. Finally, I called his wife. She told me to call him at the hospital, that he was still there. Shocked at the length of his stay, I immediately dialed his room; scared something worse had taken place.

"Hi Renee. I'm so glad you called. I wanted to let you know what happened. You didn't know, but I had a cancerous tumor the size of a grapefruit. When they opened me up it was not there. They knew how big it was and had the x-rays."

Eli paused then continued.

"There was no sign of it. They didn't know what to make of it."

Another pause.

"Yes, I know what you did. That's why I couldn't wait to tell you."

I was flabbergasted! Having no clue of his condition, I remembered specifically praying against cancer. It felt strange when the word popped out. In fact, I wondered whether it was just my imagination. Then it hit me. My obedience Sunday morning had produced a beautiful miracle of God, for His glory!

MORRIS

Morris looked up at me from his stall. He was busy wrapping bandages around a colt's sore legs. Morris was a tall man in his mid-fifties. He was loud, a voracious talker, often focusing on racism. Talking with Morris was like talking to a wall. He could see no further than himself. He knew it all and expected everyone to agree with him. Though a good caretaker of his horses, the winner's circle eluded him.

I met Morris as I met many of the race trackers, walking to and from someplace at the track. When I happened to pass his stall one day, he invited me over. We talked often after that. I tried to find common ground spiritually, but he never let on if he believed or ever had any kind of faith life.

One day Morris shocked me, saying he had walked away from his family. I asked him what that meant.

"I thought they'd be better off without me," he said nonchalantly.

"But, don't they know where you are and what you're doing?"

"Nope. Never told them. Its better that way."

Unbelieving, I tried to grasp the reasoning behind a man who shuns his wife and inheritance. Morris had no scruples. He went on with his work, like nothing was even said.

My relationship with Morris changed abruptly one day. It started out as a familiar visit, talking about our horses and how they were doing. I shared my faith in God and how much He loves horse people. Then I happened to mention a story that was in the news. It was about a man who claimed a miraculous healing.

Cynicism rose like a tiger in Morris. He not only rejected the possibility of healing but vehemently ranted and raved about holy things of God. He was treading on dangerous ground, personal feelings few people would ever vocalize.

Suddenly growing incredibly uncomfortable, I literally moved backwards. It was as though a wind was blowing us apart. I felt God's anger. He was rejecting Morris. I knew I'd never again share about God with this man. That humbling experience reminded me of Old Testament people who had walked away from a loving Creator who desired relationship with them. God's Holy Spirit power is not to be mocked.

RICHARD

A friend of one of my relatives introduced me to Richard. His wife, Sue, and their large family lived several miles from the track on acreage. He was a professional man, working at an aircraft company while still managing to train two horses. Richard was interesting and personable. I liked him because he unreservedly shared his racing 'secrets' with me. He honestly wanted horsemen the chance to be in the winners' circle, particularly those like him with little funds. It's tough not to be able to get the best trainers, riders, etc., which can be a handicap. Yet, I found overall, that it's not the money or fame that lures people like Richard. It's the sport.

Richard's bay three-year-old won her first race as a two-year-old. But this year was different. The horse had an unidentifiable problem. She placed last six races in a row. It takes a lot of guts to keep going with an animal like that. But Richard just wouldn't give up on her. He felt she was sound and some quirky thing was holding the filly back.

Up to this point, I hadn't shared much about my faith in God with Richard as he and his family were agnostics. However, Rolling Sue was ready for her seventh race and I felt compelled to pray for her. Richard's family was standing beside me when the horses burst out of the starting gate.

I looked up to the heavens and spoke aloud. "I denounce those bad races and ask you God to please let this animal do better. Amen."

Rolling Sue came out of the gate speedily and ran her heart out. She came in fourth, at least earning some prize money. Thoroughbred races pay through fifth place on a grading scale. You would have thought Rolling Sue had won, for the fans' shouts. Several people came to congratulate the family, even some trainers who marveled at the turn of events. The bible says "faith is the substance of things to be hoped for, the evidence of things not seen." Richard's persistence paid off but I believe the Almighty got his attention that day.

It was mid racing season when my relationship with Richard's wife, Sue, deepened. Since she was a relatively quiet person, I invariably found myself doing most of the talking. She seemed genuinely interested in what I said but rarely commented. My faith life tends to be an open book but Sue seemed disinterested.

That changed forever one afternoon when I invited her to a stable where my daughter's Arab was boarded. We pulled up to the huge barn and I was about to open my door when Sue broke into tears. "I want what you have," she sobbed. "How do you get it?"

Usually full of words, I was dumbstruck. This woman, who I determined, was supposedly disinterested in God was begging for relationship with Him! I was bewildered and humbled.

In the proceeding minutes, I led her through a prayer of repentance, asking God to come into her life. In a matter of seconds, peace came over Sue and she brimmed with joy. It was truly awesome to behold. Within a short time, her children followed her example and attended a church near their home. Richard saw the changes in his family but seemed unaffected.

MARNIE - A LITTLE BIT OF EDEN

She was grazing a good-looking mare beneath a giant elm tree at the north side of the track, close to the infield fence rail. I was immediately drawn to her.

"You have a nice looking mare," I said.

She smiled, a strong breeze blowing a frond of her short blond hair upward.

"You new here?" I asked.

Marnie jerked her mare, trying to keep it from nibbling the track shrubbery. "Not really." This is my first time over here. My mare was edgy this morning so I thought I'd try something new."

We talked for a long while; finally introducing ourselves.

"Yeah, I once worked for Jake, trying to learn the ropes of racetrack life. After Jake, I worked with several others, always aspiring to be a trainer. Finally earning my trainer's license, my family enabled me to start my own operation. A couple of clients came along which gave me six horses to train."

I learned Marnie and I had been brought up in the same faith but she had became disillusioned with changes in the denomination. I shared my faith life, how I received the vision of For His Glory."

"I'd like the opportunity to train Glory," she offered.

"I'm sorry. But we just gave him over to Dusty Liken. In fact, we just moved him there a couple of weeks ago. Things were getting too stressful at Jake's so we decided to move on.

Marnie nodded. "That's part of learning here and its good. Each trainer does things a little differently. You never know which key will help. Just think how lucky we are, having the privilege of being part of this special place in the world.

At that moment I wished Marnie could train Glory. But how could that ever be possible?

Marnie and I began to meet regularly.

"Want to go riding with me tonight?" she asked one morning.

A touch of anxiety hit me as I could never remember riding horses at night. Yet there was an itching to be in the saddle again.

Marnie's family had a large property in the city. They kept their young thoroughbreds there as well as a couple of riding horses. Surprisingly, it was only a few blocks from where I'd kept Pistol and Danny Boy, my first riding horses.

I will never forget that balmy evening, a full moon gazing over the hill, stars dancing in the clear skies, and a soft breeze blowing.

We saddled up the horses and wound our way through a Japanese garden, one that had been developing for three generations. I was astounded when we came to a hill with a paved creek that flowed from the top to the bottom of a 'little mountain'. It was like being in the Garden of Eden. We urged our horses upward on a special trail that ended at a padlocked gate. We found ourselves on 'top of the world,' overlooking power lines and city lights. Power lines are glory for a rider. One can run forever with no barriers in the way.

Once in the open, Marnie kicked her horse's sides and yelled, "Let's go!"

"Oh my gosh!" I said aloud.

Courageously, I went for my horse's sides too. He shot forward. Both horses ran faster and faster. I looked down, praying the animals could see where they were going and not trip. Jenny told me they see well at night and not to worry. I wasn't so sure. Oh yeah, great woman of faith!

We eventually reached the main road and walked across between oncoming cars. Up the other side of the power lines we galloped, Marnie staying in front so my horse wouldn't run off. Thankfully, the episode with Danny Boy running off had dimmed with time. I was not afraid. It was the ride of a lifetime, one I'd never forget.

After our night adventure, Marnie and I went to a local ice cream parlor and indulged. There was only a few more times to enjoy riding in this garden of delight. The family decided to sell the property and it became a city park. Now, many can enjoy what used to be for only a privileged few.

DARRYL

There would be no horseracing without exercise riders! These dedicated men and women work with their charges through thick and thin. Trainers depend on them to teach their high-strung thoroughbreds how to act on the track. They must desensitize them to noise, distractions, and a host of other things. They prepare the way so jockeys will have a 'smooth' ride. Especially challenging are the dangers inherent to two-year-olds. These courageous people help make the sport of kings happen.

"Hey Renee? Come on back! Darryl's here," shouted Jake one morning as I was leaving the barn.

Darryl Johnson, a young man in his early twenties sported shoulder length blond hair and a winning smile. His pleasant manner drew me right away. He was my first exposure to an exercise rider.

"Let's get old Glory here saddled up," quipped Jake.

I looked up, not caring much for Jake's reference to Glory as 'old'. Glory's eyes surveyed Darryl as he picked up the bridle. He didn't like his ears fiddled with and let it be known.

"Try it this way," whispered Jake. The master took the spooked gelding's attention away from the bridle. Quick as a flash, it slipped on. Darryl marveled.

It was Glory's first trip to the exercise track, a small quarter mile track across the road from the backstretch. When mastered, Glory would then go onto the main oval. I wasn't quite sure who was more nervous, Darryl, Glory or me. My hands perspired so much I stuffed them in my jean's pockets. I had anticipated this day for a long while, rehearsing in my mind the thrill of seeing 'my baby' progress further on his racing journey.

Glory leaped sideways as he entered the strange track. He went forward, only to back up and stop, his eyes blazing. Ever so slowly, Darryl coaxed him onto the track, settling him into an incredible extended trot. Hopefully, those long legs and back were a harbinger of a good runner.

Darryl would earn his money that day. His mount was a handful and it took all the knowledge he learned to keep Glory in check. That included riding the outside rail, turning into it several times to keep him from running off. My mind raced, fearing for Darryl and my horse!

Jake was suddenly at my side, watching every move by horse and rider. We all survived and after several minutes Glory was back at the barn.

"He did pretty well for the first time out. I really like Glory," said Darryl confidently.

Jake half laughed and began giving pointers for their next outing.

Finally, back at the barn, Jay and Janice hosed Glory down and tethered him to a walker. Then I filled them in on his small track debut.'

We all chatted about the challenges of racing and what things would help Glory.

"I'm grateful Jake's giving me a chance to ride," said Darryl. "I started galloping because I want to be a jockey. Would you believe the first time I got put on a horse, it ran off with me for two miles before I could stop it! The guy razzed me so bad I got on the same horse the next day and he ran off again! The third day, he told me I'd better get used to the feeling of a runaway horse or I'd never overcome my fears."

Somehow, Darryl's mentor got away with it. Despite the method, Darryl eventually learned to ride.

Getting someone to give him a chance to ride was another matter. Jake was known to help neophytes. He was no dummy and knew they'd try harder and be more available. From that day on, Darryl spent a lot of time at our stable. Glory and he had a special relationship. That made me happy and less anxious.

By mid-season Darryl and his long-time girlfriend decided to get married. They moved to another racetrack where he eventually got his jockey's license. We traveled there for his third race, which Darryl won. Being drenched by all his peers was a sight to see since it only happens when a jockey wins his first race.

Darryl later ran into some serious medical problems inherent to racing, specifically weight control. Leaving what you love can often hurt as much as the physical pain you're suffering. Darryl was between a rock and a hard place. With much sympathy from those in racing he was eventually encouraged to enter a different phase of racing. Once in a while he got on a horse 'to keep my sanity". In this way, race trackers are one big family with management and backstretch personnel working together to perpetuate the sport and help transitions.

PETE

He didn't own a horse. He didn't work at the track. Nor did he even carry any special credentials. Yet, he was intimately involved with race trackers' needs. Pete's gift of giving exceeded anyone I ever knew or met during my years at the track. A soft-spoken man with a short brown beard, Pete was mostly recognized by his captivating deep blue eyes. Their twinkle brought smiles wherever he went.

"Yes, I gamble occasionally," he once told me. "I probably could make a living at it. I once did. And I'm not perfect, just continually striving to better glorify my Creator. If I spend too much time or energy on the sport, an inner check in my spirit brings me back and I assess my motives."

Pete had an unusual gift of touching people most others shied away from; the strange, troubled people of the track were his specialty. He knew they needed more than encouragement and the normal pathways for lifestyle changes. He had a unique gift to work with the basest because they found him trustworthy.

One day, I was looking for Pete when I happened to cut through a particular shed row. The trainer in that stable was a tough looking woman whom I had never met and knew little about. Her groom was a man with strange hollow eyes that always looked down. Since no one seemed to be around that morning, I quickly walked past the stalls toward another stable. A sudden move on my right caught my attention. The man with the hollow eyes was standing on something at the back of the stall and 'doing it'. Bestiality was barely a word in my vocabulary. Most everyone knows it exists. The incredulity of the sight overwhelmed me. Grateful the man didn't see me, I beat it out of that stable.

Still in shock, I decided to stop at the track cafeteria. There was Pete. One look at my ashen face told him something was wrong.

"Renee. Some perversion is so base you can't help a person. They refuse to abandon their darkness and poverty to reach for the light. God is sad, too, you know."

I realized Pete had tried to reach this man. I didn't want to believe his words, though I knew better. My optimistic nature resists the knowledge that anyone would purposely refuse God's gift of salvation.

For many days afterward, my spirit grieved for that reprobate man. I thank God for men like Pete who are God's earthly angels. Pete was given the power to touch the untouchable; but in the end he had to accept defeat. The deadly choice of that man to stay in his perversion prevailed over the choice God gave him for forgiveness and freedom. Although we do have free will I thought about his eternal soul, the day he would have to face his Creator. The bible says it is a fearful thing to fall in the hands of the living God, to hear the words "I never knew you."

DEFENDING EVANGELIST BILLY GRAHAM

As winter faded into spring, colorful crocuses peeked out of the earth. So was the track vibrant with activity. New people crossed the screen of our lives at an ever-increasing rate. Sadly, our once strong relationship with Jake deteriorated. His dark attitudes bred uneasiness in me and I found myself begging God to take us in a different direction. A short time later, one of Jake's grooms quit to work with a trainer named Mac. My visits there grew longer and longer. If only Jake were like Mac.

Next to Mac's barn was a seventy-year-old trainer named Jenkin Salas. I mused how he whipped around his horses with the energy of someone half his age. Bill was a tall lithe man with graying hair and steel blue eyes. Eventually, I struck up a conversation with his wife, Carlene. a petite frail woman with severe arthritis. Carlene was constantly at her husband's side, doing what she could to help in the training of their two horses. I mentioned Mac and my desire to change trainers.

"We've known Mac for a long time," she said. "He has very good help, which I consider most important."

Her husband Bill walked by and broke into the conversation. "Will you wrap this horse's leg, dear?"

"Right away, honey," she replied. "Oh, this is Renee."

Bill nodded, barely a hint of a smile escaping his thin lips. I had a strange feeling Bill was a very self-centered person, caring for no one, except perhaps his horses and Carlene.

For the next few weeks, I chitchatted more and more with Carlene. Finally, I felt comfortable enough to talk with her about God. She said nothing the first few times I broached the subject. One day she suddenly blurted out, "I believe in God! I have also seen a vision of Jesus Christ!"

Stunned, I asked, "Will you tell me about it?"

"Well…. It's hard to describe."

"Carlene?" interrupted Bill.

Carlene instantly walked away, as if I had never been there, as if our conversation never was! It was apparent she was a very submissive woman under a very demanding husband.

The next time I saw Carlene, she was washing down a horse after its morning workout. "I'd like to tell you about the story of my horse, For His Glory."

She angrily replied, "I don't believe God's at the racetrack! Nor does He have anything to do with it!"

"Then how can you be a believer and still work here?" I questioned.

Carlene chose not to answer. Nor did she budge from her strong conviction the next few times we met. I was unable to persuade her that God was truly interested in racetrack people and their animals. Finally, I let go of the subject and we were back to our usual chitchatting.

Bill rarely said anything, only once grunting to display his contempt of religion. I tried to stay away from the subject. One morning, though, my exuberance bubbled over, the result of a wonderful experience with a visiting evangelist the previous night. I went headlong into the story, thinking only Carlene was listening.

Bill suddenly appeared, his face livid with rage! "They're all shysters, those so-called evangelists, especially taking people's money, like that Billy Graham!"

My dander rose. Bill hit fertile soil for I had just read a series of articles about Dr. Graham's life and business practices. Any pointing of the finger at this godly man, I could now refute with facts. Challenging this accuser was not an option.

"Bill, if you were the owner of a business that made ten million dollars a year, then how much would you take for yourself?" I asked.

"What has that to do with anything?" he replied and continued to rant on.

I braced myself and replied, "Most of us would feel we deserved a good portion of it, especially if we were away from our families several months a year and were constantly in the public eye, every area of our life being constantly scrutinized."

Bill's eyes blazed and he raised his fist. "Look at that Jim Jones. He hoodwinked poor people with his hunger for money and power!"

I paused, feeling sorry for Bill. Yes, Jim Jones was a good example of people swayed by a personality, even giving up their lives, but that isn't all men of God. The bible says a man is a fool who believes there is no God. It seemed Bill did not believe in God, only in himself. I pondered how one could come to that conclusion.

A question suddenly popped into my mind. "Bill, do you believe all race track people are dishonest, conniving and deceitful? I've found evidence quite to the contrary."

Bill grew quiet, as if a chord pierced his hard shell. I prayed fervently, hoping another blow might break through this old man's cold heart.

"Don't you believe there are any good people at the track?" I repeated.

Bill skirted the issue but answered, "What are the facts about Billy Graham?

"Billy Graham takes only about five percent of his earnings. I think that is very conservative for someone who could demand millions. People who only went to one meeting still get material from his headquarters years later and they never even gave a nickel. Dr. Graham's desire to stay in contact with those who have responded to his ministry reaches far beyond what most people would expect. Would a trainer do that for a client that moved on to another trainer? Once you leave town, you figure it's the other person's problem."

Bill humped his shoulders. I could only hope he thought a little more about his preconceived notions.

Kindly waving, I left the barn, wondering what Carlene thought of our exchange.

It was several days later before I visited Bill and Carlene again. She was stooping down, rubbing her horse with liniment, and then rubbing it on her own body.

"With all my aches and pains, it is the only relief I get," she said nonchalantly.

I thought the practice a little strange, maybe even dangerous, but said nothing. DMSO is a common liniment for horses and very strong. Carlene was an arthritis sufferer and I realized she was probably mobile because of the liniment. How people like her endured grueling days and severe weather conditions with dogged perseverance was more than I could imagine. Ironically, a short time later, a national television show said DMSO, the cure-all for horse aches and pains, was being refined for humans and with no side effects. Ah! Horse people knew the secret already.

Toward the end of the season, Bill and Carlene began to attend Glory's races. We became good friends and I will always remember them, especially their candid questions and dedication to the horse industry. I could only hope that one day Bill might know the joy of a life of faith.

SHORTY'S DECISION

Life was very exciting taking care of Glory daily and keeping aware of the progress of John's Vision. In my spare time I kept working with Anna and also saw the budding of Monica, who was preparing her filly for 4-H classes. Although Veronica was allergic to horses, she eventually was able to ride Anna for a short time. Thankfully, she was kept busy with piano lessons so she too could use her talent.

By this time, I was used to seeing a mother often drop off her young daughter at Shorty's, supposedly to ride horses. I tried to look the other way but someone finally told me about their relationship. I tried to ignore an inner voice telling me to address the situation. Instead, I endeavored to talk to him about God.

"I believe in God, even had dreams of seeing the future death of people I knew."

Although unusual, Shorty's response did not particularly alarm me. Most people, he said, were scared to death when he spoke of this.

As he sat hunched back in an old beaten-up chair, my eyes turned toward the wall behind him. A strange sense came over me, that even the walls seemed dead. I promised myself to bring a picture to bring in new life. However, my greatest challenge at the moment was how to bring this little old man an ultimatum. The inner gnawing in my gut wouldn't stop if I didn't speak. No one wants to be responsible for someone's soul, but sometimes the Almighty chooses to intervene in the affairs of men.

"You know how much I care for this family and the desire of my heart is to have you walk with God....but you have to give up this girlfriend or else your salvation is in danger," I said with trepidation.

His eyes met mine as he nodded, saying he'd think on it.

My heart sank when he finally told me 'no'. Shorty had money, horses, wonderful friends, but you can't take them with you into the next world. A loving God may overlook our naivety but He also will warn us about sin that endangers our soul.

In spite of my concern for Shorty, I still managed to put in a word or two to his son Pete about God. But it was his girlfriend, Joanie, who would have a profound effect on his life. Although he had a tendency to put her down, he respected Joanie's sensitivity and intelligence, that they both needed God since each had only one parent and seemed not to have friends besides each other. They felt a void and although I could not relate to what they were going through, God was drawing them to Himself. They began to attend church to try and find where they belonged and where they might grow in their new faith.

Whether Shorty ever repented of his sin I will never know but God was faithful to send someone to let him know what he was supposed to do in his life to prepare himself for His Creator. He died a short time later.

FROM A JOCKEY'S PERSPECTIVE
(Interview given by permission)

Darryl Wyman stiffened as he twisted a piece of For His Glory's coarse black mane around his hands. The big horse had a habit of leaping too high out of the starting gate, losing precious seconds and making a dump easily possible. Every bit of strength and mental acumen would be needed just to stay on the nearly seventeen hand gelding. A wipeout or dump at the gate would be disastrous!

Darryl loved the feel of this horse, its extraordinary long neck and back. Except for protruding bones, which made him appear malnourished, Glory stood out in the crowd. So, what if people stared at his bony structure. This was his Darryl's chance to ride in a race and that's all that mattered.

He tried to settle in the saddle, but Glory swayed, lifting his left foot then his right. The horse next to him snorted and twitched his ears nervously. Only number nine was holding up the race. The track crowd grew quiet, waiting for the chutes to open.

Glory suddenly reared and Darryl ducked just in time. A broken nose was not on his agenda! A replay from two weeks before flashed through his mind. He was on a two-year-old filly that reared continuously during gate certification. If the filly refused to cooperate by the fifth try, she would not be allowed to race. Darryl was willing to try an extra time, more for pride's sake than the filly's, which proved a mistake. She caught him as her head lunged forward, than back. His nose bled and he looked like a mess. Thankfully, his nose healed quickly though some bruising still remained.

"Easy Glory, come on, whoa now." Darryl's soothing voice calmed the gelding and he relaxed. Darryl took a deep breath and bit his lip. "Concentrate, just concentrate," he thought. All that mattered was staying on and letting this horse show what he could do. A quick glance at Jake meant he had better have his wits about him. Jake was tough to work for; but Darryl, like everyone else, appreciated the veteran's knowledge. Jake gave new guys a break. That made him popular with new jockeys. Nevertheless, a bad ride could mean another rider if Glory showed any potential at all.

Darryl took a deep breath and bit his lip. This was the final exam, the climax of three grueling years learning to ride. Nothing could match the exhilaration of entering the great oval. Of that much, he was sure. He often dreamed of being photographed in the winner's circle. Could Glory be the horse? He wasn't sure. The dreams were surreal.

As for Renee, she was a nice owner to work with despite always talking about God. He did have to agree that several 'coincidences' gave him this opportunity to ride. He wasn't sure, but just maybe there was really something to this God business. Renee said she was inspired to buy Glory. This was strange language to a guy who had no religious background. But everyone had a right to their own opinion, as long as he was paid!

"Glory, it's your day to make your owner proud." Glory's ears flicked back. He knew Darryl's whisper. "Now just take it easy and stay near to the ground and we'll lick em."

The flag went up after the last gate clinked loudly. The familiar lump in Darryl's throat grew bigger by the moment. Would the sleepless nights trying to find the key to stop Glory leaping from the gate prove of any value? He hoped so.

Glory didn't have the breeding quality of the other horses but his size and heart could prove a factor. Horse and rider must sync to give them a shot at the money.

Hidden actions behind the starting gate ended when the bell rang. The chutes opened and a burst of horseflesh coming from captivity now made the audience captive.

"And they're off!" roared the track announcer.

Glory leaped high into the air. Darryl almost lost the hunk of mane; but he finally settled in and went with his horse. That high jump cost them. Glory was in last place. He urged the big gelding forward, sure these five short furlongs would feel more like a mile. Glory responded to his hands. That was a good sign.

Darryl remembered the first time he rode. It was at a private farm on a quarter mile track. "Can you ride at all, kid?" the trainer had asked.

"Oh yeah, sure can. I ride ranch horses and lots of bareback."

"Okay, I'll put you on this here gelding."

Darryl jumped at the chance. He ran to buy boots at the tack shop and a new helmet. His old helmet bit the dust one too many times.

The trainer had saddled the gelding by the time he jogged back to the barn. It was a warm spring morning, the sun barely topping the mountain beyond the track. Birds chirped loudly from a grove of fruit trees. It seemed like a picture perfect day; but a nightmare loomed ahead.

"Here you go," said the trainer as he heaved Darryl into the saddle.

Soon on the track, the trainer let loose of the bridle. Butterflies suddenly arose in Darryl's throat. He almost went limp. Recovering his composure, he felt the horse ease from a walk to an extended trot. The gelding seemed gentle. That was exactly what Darryl needed. However, the track suddenly appeared longer and wider than it really was. Even the ground seemed further away! Without thinking, he took a heavy hold of the reins and felt the horse ease further into the bit. "What's this horse doing?" he thought and tried to pull back. Instead, the gelding lengthened his stride and was soon racing. Darryl hung on with all his might, hoping it would miraculously stop. But it didn't!

Around and around the track he flew, feeling weaker by the moment. The trainer just grinned as he passed.

"If I could only breathe," he thought. His fingers froze as he gasped for breath. His nineteen years flashed before him. He was too weak to pull back and the gelding seemed to be enjoying his sport. He remembered jockeys stand up in the saddle after they go past the finish line. Nevertheless, he could not move. His ankles felt like cement in the stirrups and his back was killing him.

His face stung as dirt hit and ground into his cheeks, the result of an early morning shower.

It was now or never. At least there wasn't anyone on the track except the laughing trainer. If he jumped off, he'd he be free of this brute beast and maybe even come out alive. He made a rolling dive and hit the ground with a thud. His elbow hit a rock which made him groan but at least he could breathe. He picked himself up in time to see the gelding running back toward the trainer. What kind of trainer would let this happen? he moaned. Next thing he knew, the trainer was helping him up, apologizing for the hard ride.

"Hey, you didn't give me any lessons on this here horse," Darryl said meekly.

The tall black haired trainer just grinned. "Well, listen here. Tomorrow morning you come back at 5:00am and I'll let you try Old Smokie one more time. Then I'll see if you got it in you to be a jockey."

Darryl wiped off his pants and hobbled over to a bench. Old Smokey? A strange feeling crept over him. He had survived the runaway and come out mostly unscathed. There was still some spirit left. He would give himself another chance. Besides, the stubborn streak his mother always nagged him about might actually work in his favor.

I'll be there," he said confidently.

The trainer, who was laughing once again, walked the sweating gelding back to the barn.

Darryl needed a cold soda. In fact, he might need three after this ordeal.

FOR HIS
GLORY

A TRIBUTE TO RACEHORSE PEOPLE

JOCKEYS

A special breed destined to sit atop the horse and bring it to its fullest potential. They are bold, daring, and single minded men and women with disciplined bodies and tough hearts to withstand the wins, defeats, and injuries inherent to their profession.

TRAINERS

Men and women with iron bodies who have the final authority to see that horses are taken care of in all their needs and challenges. Their trained eyes see the intricacies and uniqueness of each animal. They are responsible to their clients and aware of the needs of their help.

GROOMS

Dedicated ones who are attuned to the horses put in their care. They must be on call up to 24 hours a day. They stabilize their charges and help them through their fears, pains, and triumphs. Though low paid for the hours put in, they remain optimistic "their" animals will bring in a paycheck.

EXERCISE RIDERS

With a love of riding they persevere through rain, sleet, heat, bucking, jumping, tripping, falling, and sailing through the breeze at 5:00AM. They are likely to know if their mount is especially gifted, maybe even Kentucky Derby or Breeders Cup contenders.

FARRIERS

Destined to provide the foundation of an animal without which there would be no race. They have nerves of steel and a commanding tongue. Their hands and fingers are wrought with remembrances of past failures and brute beasts. Eventually numbed by much criticism, they get the blame for troubled feet yet keep trucking on.

VETERINARIANS

Men and women who cannot always live up to their role as miracle workers but who feel for the animal and help defeat the enemies of the horse. Sickness and disease, bone and birth problems all fall into the laps of these people who pay the price in education to administer the above and beyond of everyday equine problems.

PONY RIDERS

Faithful ones who have to have an iron hand to hold their charges on their early morning gallop. They and their horses are vital for runners before and after races.

TACK SUPPLIERS

Industrious at providing equipment, medicines, garments, coffee and a friendly atmosphere for the many workers around the great oval.

GATE CREW

Your tales about getting horses in and out of the starting gate involves a lot of working with horse tails! Danger is a way of life to you and the comedy that goes on behind the scenes keeps you going and your insurance agents wary!

HAY, FEED, CLEAN-UP PERSONNEL

You truck in and truck out in relentless pursuit of the choicest available products in order to satisfy customers. Cleanup crew people are welcome sights as you make it possible to have a healthy environment. A friendly smile is your reward.

CONCESSION AND RESTAURANTS WORKERS

Young and older workers on the front and backstretch who make their living pleasing patrons with food and drinks. Many a professional started their career through this service.

RACING OFFICIALS

Given the task of organizing, directing, estimating and providing a wholesome atmosphere where fairness prevails. Though not always perfect, they are sensitive to all needs, knowing their lives are built around deadlines.

AGENTS

Hustling mounts for their jockeys, they cover a multitude of miles on foot, dodging the angry looks of trainers who for one reason or another did not get who they asked for.

OWNERS

Special people, who once they get into the business, have a hard time ever leaving it! They put up with a lot of excuses, some abuses, but hopefully triumph in the end with a trip to the winner's circle and a photo for posterity. Without their money and support the industry would not be.

BREEDERS

A science and an art, breeders spend countless hours studying pedigrees to find the "best" sires to send their mares to. There is great fulfillment seeing their progeny become successful.

RACETRACK OWNERS AND PERSONNEL

Without your ownership and work on the front side of the track, the horse could not manifest its destiny and the Sport of Kings would be no more! Your livelihood is supported by the public and those on the backside to produce a good economy.

PRESS, COMMUNICATIONS, AUDIO

Behind the scenes, yet informing the horsemen and women, trainers, breeders, and world of what goes on at the great oval. Few of the public would deny they follow the wins or losses of the newspaper analyst. With his imaginary money he tries to beat the odds by getting through a season with money left. A peak at yesterday's performance soothes nerves at the off-limits audio-visual room where the angles count.

BETTORS

You take your hard earned money to make wagers based on the racing form, jockey or jockey silks, best decorated horse, knowing the owner, trainer, groom, etc. or just get a gut feeling. The fact is you enjoy taking a chance on an animal that has been bred for the ultimate purpose of achieving its fullest potential and you make that possible.

ABOUT THE AUTHOR

Rita H. Joyce was born in Seattle, Washington, graduating from Franklin High School. She attended some classes at the University of Washington, but her college career was curtailed when a home emergency forced her to go to work to help support her family. She has a birth daughter, an adopted daughter, five stepchildren, and is twice widowed. Following her dreams led her and her second husband to move to Florida in 2000, where she has lived ever since.

Joyce is the author of three self-published books – Her first (*Gozzy Goose's Christmas Gift*) (e-book only) was chosen in 2002 for the Under Nine Literacy Promotion at Universal Cineplex, City Walk, Universal Studios and promoted as one of the *Stories From the Silver Screen!* A limited revised edition was also self-published in 2015 but is out of print. Two sequels were written but not published. There was also a Read-Along CD with an original song that is being considered for release as a DVD.

A third edition of Joyce's "*Johnny Peppertoes*" includes her newly formed company "Rita's Publishing". Originally self-published, it was used for three years in the fourth grade curriculum at a school in her hometown of Kissimmee, Florida. The Principal of the school acknowledged after the third year that "Peppertoes" was responsible for the highest scores ever in their reading classes. A lesson plan is available if desired. A movie is in the initial stages of development. A short video clip is an on-line presence, especially through Amazon.

Joyce's third self-published book is "Wandawillie," presently available on Amazon. It was inspired by a newspaper article about a visiting kangaroo. As is Gozzy Goose, Wandawillie is a rhyming story.

Rita's current project is producing a Memoir, an unusual story of much of her early life, including thirteen years on the backstretch of a thoroughbred racetrack. Her inspiration for this book included knowing the name of the racehorse, its stable name, and other events before they ever happened. Another book in progress features the paintings of her late friend Delores Korenko. It is about a snoopy fawn.

Joyce's talents include song writing. Her repertory of music includes rap, soft rock, country, and sacred music. Her present endeavor is completing a two-year soft rock song that relays an experience she, her husband and two children had one night as they watched a full moon.

A music video will follow. A rap song about to be released by Corey Eugene Mathis addresses the effects of alcohol abuse. Two of her songs feature the work of an orchestral maestro from South America, though not yet available to the public. She has also written a song for Johnny Peppertoes.

Joyce is expectant of one of her literary works being made into a TV series.

Rita H. Joyce
407-201-8812 messages only

AUTHOR'S OTHER BOOKS

When a hidden jump rope causes Johnny Ashton to stumble into nasty blackberry bushes, he takes vengeance on the family of neighbor twins Callie and Laurie.

After an ambulance comes screeching to the house with sirens blaring and the driver announcing a fire at the mill, Johnny sneaks into the back of his father's work truck. Once there, they hear there are people trapped inside!

What will Johnny do? Johnny wakes suddenly during the first night in his new tree house. What he sees through the window will bring him to a place he never imagined and requires great courage!

When immigrant Irish brothers Tom and Nathan O'Reilly move into the 'haunted' house behind the Ashton's, Johnny is determined to make friends with them. He learns about their culture as they learn about his secret "problem." During the Plainsville Independence Day celebration, the three friends find themselves in a frightening predicament.

To save the town, Johnny "Peppertoes" Ashton must overcome his greatest fear.

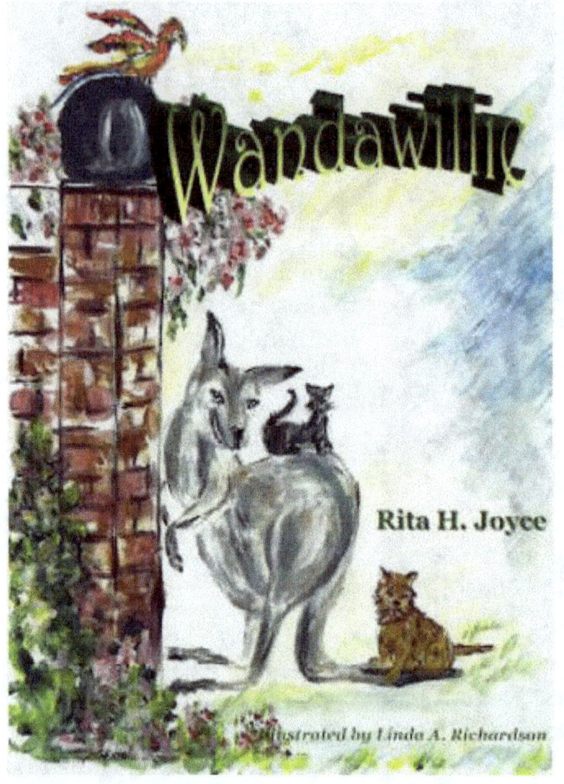

Wandawillie was inspired by a visiting kangaroo to my home town.

I am not and was never into witches but love fairy tales. As the rhyme evolved, I was able to accept this strange calling to write as there is religious significance to monk's salt.

That became very apparent as I was reading one of my books to a young girl. She was going through a very traumatic time in her life. Special prayer and a little bag of salt was all she needed to grow into a healthy young lady.

A rhyming tale of a goose from Toulouse that lays golden eggs at Christmas time. After being snatched by a falcon, Gozzy leaves behind a surprising gift for the townspeople.

This tale, however, is not the end of Gozzy's story!